"Adam...touch

Something seemed t... glided his hand back up to cup her breast, rubbing a teasing thumb over the nipple and Eva shuddered.

Acting on instinct, Eva urgently bunched her nightgown up to the tops of her thighs and straddled him.

Adam pushed her away slightly and removed his glasses. Eva was too filled with need to concentrate on anything more than the ball of heat spiraling within her. Adam's fingers dug into the flesh of her thighs and hauled her forward until she rested against his arousal. The action forced a gasp from Eva's throat. The knowledge that there was nothing more than his underwear and her nightgown separating them further fed the fire within her...until a rush of awareness made her notice that *nothing more than his underwear and her nightgown separated them.*

Eva rested her forehead against his cheek. "This is insane."

Adam took her face in his hand. "I gotta tell you, Eva, if that's what's going to happen if we have to kiss in front of your family, I think we should avoid it at all costs."

Dear Reader,

"How do you two write together?" is the question most asked of us as a husband-and-wife writing team. Our response is invariably "*very* carefully."

Joking aside, we couldn't have plotted a more ideal situation for our characters, much less ourselves. In our books you'll see a little bit of both of us, a whole lot of imagination and a genuine love for what we do. In *Constant Craving*, we didn't have to go too far to research Eva's Greek-American background because Tony himself is Greek-American. And Adam and Eva's situation somewhat resembles the circumstances surrounding our own leap into marital bliss eleven years ago. No, no, Tony isn't an F.B.I. agent, and Lori wasn't…well, you'll see what we mean. Anyway, this story isn't about us, although as our first book, it holds a special place in our hearts. No, it's about Adam and Eva and the sizzling trail they must blaze to find forever.

We call Toledo, Ohio, home base, but go back "home" to Greece as often as we can. We'd love to hear from you. Write to P.O. Box 12271, Toledo, OH 43612. Please include a self-addressed stamped envelope for a reply. Or visit the web site we share with other Temptation authors at www.temptationauthors.com.

Here's wishing you romance, love and happiness!

Lori & Tony Karayianni
aka Tori Carrington

CONSTANT CRAVING
Tori Carrington

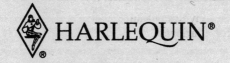

HARLEQUIN®

TORONTO • NEW YORK • LONDON
AMSTERDAM • PARIS • SYDNEY • HAMBURG
STOCKHOLM • ATHENS • TOKYO • MILAN • MADRID
PRAGUE • WARSAW • BUDAPEST • AUCKLAND

We lovingly dedicate this to Elizabeth Bevarly, Barbara "Buzzie" Kelly, Linda Markowiak, Teresa Medeiros and Cathy Snodgrass, whose generosity of spirit and wisdom helped lift us to this magical point; to the Romance Writers of America and Maumee Valley RWA for their unwavering support and guidance on our quest; to our sisters- and brothers-in-arms on Genie's RomEx and RWAlink for their compassion; and to Brenda Chin and Birgit Davis-Todd for welcoming us into the Harlequin family and proving that dreams really can come true. Heartfelt thanks to you all.

ISBN 0-373-25816-X

CONSTANT CRAVING

1

GOD, THAT WOMAN has a great pair of legs. The sort of legs that could bring a man to his knees just imagining them wrapped around his waist.

Adam Grayson shifted the telephone receiver from his ear and leaned forward to stare through the crack in his door. Eva Burgess, the only person visible in the hall of Sheffert, Logan and Brace, Certified Public Accountants, was pouring hot water from the coffee machine into a hefty mug. Her dark hair was pulled back in an ever-present twist. The clean lines of her pale green business suit tried but failed to hide her tantalizing curves. But it was her legs—shapely and long and drop-dead sexy, despite her low-heeled shoes—that were the stuff of which fantasies were made. Adam tugged at his collar. Had the air-conditioning buckled under the unusual September heat, or had his own cooling system gone on the fritz?

Eva briefly met his gaze, little more than a flash of her eyes, before she quickly turned away.

"Grayson, you still there?" Weckworth gruffly muttered as Adam pressed the receiver back to his ear.

"Yeah, I'm here." Which was a damn shame. He'd much rather be drifting somewhere off the coast of Jamaica on his thirty-five-foot sailboat, Eva Burgess stretched out on deck, the hot, exotic sun melting away her truckload of inhibitions and tingeing her skin with color.

Adam swiveled his chair around, away from the

door and junior partner Eva Burgess. He rubbed his forehead, censuring himself for lusting after a woman who was supposed to be one of his superiors. Especially since a few days before she'd turned down his dinner invitation. Though his come-on had little to do with Eva's legs, and more to do with what she knew about her wily boss, her rejection had bothered Adam in a way that wasn't in the least professional.

John Weckworth cursed in his ear. "You've been at that place too long. You're starting to act like an accountant. Did you even hear a word I said?"

"I *am* an accountant," Adam reminded John.

"You may be a CPA, but you're no ordinary accountant, Grayson. You're one of the best field agents in the FBI Financial Crimes Unit. Big difference."

Maybe. Adam stared at a boring sketch he'd inherited three weeks earlier from Oliver Pinney, his office's previous occupant. He lowered his voice to prevent anyone from overhearing. "Anyway, yes, I got what you said. You told me you can't justify keeping me on the job any longer."

"Nada, nothing, zip. That's what three weeks of trying to nail Sheffert for tax evasion has gotten us. You're losing it, Grayson. Two years ago, you would have had Sheffert strung up by the shorts in a week."

"Yeah, and two years ago I was infiltrating militia groups trying to figure out who was actually financing their adventures. Not some nickel-and-dime accounting firm whose senior partner happens to have a couple of criminal friends and knows how to hide his dirty laundry."

"Don't forget, he also knows how to hide a body or two—that is, if Pinney's ever shows up," John said. "Now, you got anything on this guy, or should I pull you out?"

Adam straightened his blue-and-red-striped tie, half of him wanting to tell Weckworth to shut down the entire operation. He'd had it with playing Adam Gardner, the socially challenged CPA. And he was especially tired of hiding behind a pair of geeky glasses and cheesy, off-the-rack business suits. Besides, the day marked the beginning of Labor Day weekend and Norman Sheffert was off to the Cape until Tuesday. Adam had already tapped out his sources at Dun & Bradstreet Corp. in New York, finding no trace of the usual a.k.a.'s for any of Sheffert's clients, or hidden assets. And his use of the program NetMap on Sheffert's main computer had also failed to turn up any evidence of collusion and fraud.

Still...

Adam's muscles bunched and he rolled his shoulders, admitting that despite the drawbacks of the assignment, the blasted competitive side of him refused to admit defeat. And there was the fact that he'd yet to gain exclusive access to two key accounts: Honeycutt and Rockwood. Not that he expected to find anything useful in them. The rest of the accounts he'd reviewed had been so remarkably clean, he'd been surprised they hadn't reeked of virtual detergent.

He scratched his chin. There *was* that one little avenue left unexplored by way of Eva Burgess, Sheffert's right-hand gal. Besides, if he left, he couldn't enjoy ogling her legs anymore.

He bit back a curse. John was right. He *was* losing it.

"Look, John—"

Someone rapped lightly on the door frame. He swung around to find Eva standing there, smiling anxiously.

"Sorry," she said quickly. "I didn't realize you were on the phone."

Adam snapped up in his chair and waved her in. He

didn't try to check his surprise. Eva hadn't come to his office once in the past three weeks. "No problem, I'm almost done here. Come in and have a seat."

"Grayson? Damn it, what's going on? Are we still having a conversation or what?" Weckworth's voice echoed from the receiver.

Adam ignored John's baiting question and concentrated instead on Eva.

If he didn't know better, he'd think she was nervous about something. But nothing rattled Eva Burgess. He watched her smooth down the side of her suit jacket several times before finally stepping toward the cafeteria-like chair in front of his desk. She put her steaming mug on his desk, then shifted the mountain of files on top of the chair to the floor. Adam fought not to eye the way she tugged on the hem of her skirt to keep it from riding up as she crossed those marvelous legs.

"Grayson?" Weckworth barked.

Adam budged his gaze to stare into Eva's face. He honestly didn't know what intrigued him about the woman. She wasn't his type. Sure, she had a lot going for her in the looks department, but he met enough challenges in his career. For that reason alone he preferred flirty types who knew the power of their femininity. The sort of women who were undemanding when he moved on, as he always did, for reasons he told himself were professional...though even he admitted to questioning those arguments lately.

Still, he'd never dated a dynamic ice queen of Eva's caliber. He didn't plan to, either. Life was too short.

He grimaced. Then why did he want to jump in a cold shower every time he saw her?

Eva must have taken his silence to mean she should speak, for she quietly cleared her throat.

"I need a favor, Adam. A big favor. Will you...I

mean, can you…" She drew a deep breath, then blurted, "Marry me…tonight?"

Adam nearly dropped the telephone. Every last thought in his head rushed out, leaving him uncommonly speechless. His gaze brushed Eva from head to toe. He searched for a sign that this was some sort of bad joke, a candid-camera prank that would leave him looking the fool.

Eva Burgess appeared dead serious.

Coughing, Adam dragged the receiver back to his mouth, purposely keeping his words ambiguous. "Uh…I'll call you back."

The tinny sound of Weckworth's voice echoed through the otherwise silent room as Adam missed the cradle once before finally hanging up the receiver.

He sat forcefully back in his chair, causing the springs to give a punctuating squeak. Had Eva Burgess said what he thought she'd said? He narrowed his eyes. He'd come across many a bold proposal in his time, but this outranked them all.

He couldn't resist a hesitant grin. "Don't you think we should try dinner first?"

She blinked at him, eyeing the relaxed, unperturbed way he sprawled in the chair. Instantly, Adam sat straight. For a moment the baffling woman had made him forget his role. *Big* mistake.

"Uh, sorry, it's just that what you said…well, I must have been hearing things, because I could swear you just asked me to marry you and…" Adam let his sentence drift off into a hesitant never-never land. A tactic that worked well even for a geek. It placed the other person in the position of finishing.

A warm blush colored Eva's cheeks.

"That didn't quite come out the way I planned. I…" She gestured with her hands. Hands that usually stayed clasped before her, whether on her desk, or at the conference table. Adam found her gesturing more natural. "I don't mean that I *literally* want you to marry me. That would be—"

"Ludicrous," he supplied.

A wary shadow darkened her eyes. "Yes. It would be ludicrous. I mean, we haven't even known each other three weeks, and then only at work."

She suddenly stopped and Adam stomped down the urge to apply the silent treatment to get her to spill more. He used his index finger to push the bridge of his glasses up on his nose. "Then what is it you are asking me...exactly?"

Her throat contracted as she swallowed. "I need someone to be my husband this weekend. I mean, someone to play the part of my husband."

Adam eyed her. "I see. And, naturally, I'm the first person you thought of for the role."

She frowned and smoothed back her already smooth hair. "The fourth, actually. If it helps any, you are the first I've asked." Her cheeks burned a bright scarlet. "I've been putting together a speech all day, and for the life of me, I can't remember a single word of it." She smiled, obviously frazzled. Not at all like the woman he'd come to know. "You see, my mother called this morning. My father's ill...how ill, I'm not sure. But it must be serious for my mother to summon me home. Anyway, I promised to come tomorrow. My mother ended the conversation saying she looked forward to seeing me and...well, my husband."

Adam carefully listened to her words. What did any of this have to do with him? In all honesty, he hadn't known Eva Burgess was married. She didn't wear a ring, and still wasn't, a quick glance verified. No one around the firm knew much about her private life. Not that that surprised him. When he'd asked her out, her refusal had been about as warm as an Arctic wind.

And any attempts at forming a casual friendship with her around the coffee machine had earned him little more than one-sided polite chitchat. On his side.

She had to be in dire straits indeed to have shared that much of herself with him.

Adam pulled on the tail of his tie and tried to work his way around his surprise.

"Then I'd say it would be a good idea to take your husband," he said carefully. She dropped her gaze. "You do have a husband, don't you?"

"Yes. I mean no." She reached for her mug on the desktop, nearly spilling the contents of what he guessed was tea as she lifted the cup to her lips. She appeared to have difficulty swallowing. "At least I did. We...our divorce was recently finalized."

Adam felt an instant twinge of relief. She was divorced. Good. No possessive husband to worry about when they sailed off into the wild blue yonder for a weekend of hot sex. He picked up a pencil and tapped it against the desk, feigning a fumble that sent the pencil flying to the floor in front of Eva. She put her cup down and bent to retrieve the pencil. The crisp V neck of her white blouse under her jacket bowed open, giving the briefest, tiniest flash of creamy lace. Adam stifled a groan.

She handed the pencil back to him.

"I see. Your parents don't know about your recent difficulties?" he murmured.

His gaze must have lingered a little longer than he intended for she tugged at the lapels of her jacket, pulling them tightly together over her blouse. "No. No, they don't. My parents live in Louisiana. A place some seventy miles southwest of New Orleans. The town's little more than a bayou village called Belle Rivage. Not exactly nearby."

Louisiana? Adam arched an eyebrow. He was usually pretty good with accents, but hadn't pegged hers. She must have moved to Jersey some time ago and made a conscious effort to train the accent out of her throaty voice.

"My family has never met Bill—that's my ex-husband—in case you're wondering how I could pull this off."

Adam committed the name to memory.

Eva leaned forward earnestly. "Look, I know this is a lot to ask, but if you agree to play the role of my husband, I promise you won't have to stay longer than a day. I'll explain you have to get back to work, and keep you away from the family as much as possible. I'll foot all the expenses, of course, and even include a side trip to New Orleans if you'd like. A bonus, of sorts, for doing this for me."

Adam toyed with his tie, hoping she would buy the nervous gesture. He considered the opportunity she just handed him. At a virtual dead end in his attempts to get any damning evidence against Norman Sheffert, Eva was opening a door he was loath to close. She was his last hope in this investigation. Being in close contact with her for twenty-four hours meant he would have access not only to her personal effects, but to her and whatever knowledge she had of her employer's illegal dealings.

Besides, taking her up on her offer meant spending more time near the woman herself.

Adam hesitated. Accepting the offer too hastily would not only put his undercover status at risk. He had little doubt it would make him suspect in Eva's eyes as well, despite her urgent behavior.

"I...don't quite know how to respond to this," he said, pretending an interest in straightening the business cards in a holder on his desk. "In the words of Spock, this request of yours is highly illogical."

The beginnings of a smile softened her harried expression. "Why doesn't it surprise me that you quote Spock?"

Adam feigned a wounded expression.

"Sorry," she said quickly. "Anyway, I know how… illogical my proposal is. And I don't think I've gone about this in a very direct way, either. But I hadn't anticipated this situation and, well, I'm not very good at putting plans together so fast."

He looked up from his business cards. "Well, if I say yes, this is one way of getting my date with you, isn't it?"

Eva's gaze flicked over his face and for a moment he thought she could see right through him. "Actually, if you do agree to do this favor for me, Adam, I must insist you not try anything…personal. I'm—" she cleared her throat "—I'm not looking for a relationship with any man. I think it's better we get that straight right now."

Adam watched the way she thumbed the base of her bare ring finger. "Until now, I had everything perfectly straight. But I am a bit thrown, what with your proposal of marriage and all. Even if it *is* only for a day."

A bit thrown? Hell, she'd floored him, despite his eleven years as an agent. And despite his two-month relationship—or as close as he came to a relationship, anyway—with off-Broadway tap dancer Julia Springer, whose mission in life was apparently to shock him and everybody else she came across. It hadn't surprised him at all when she up and broke things off two days after he started dressing like a geeky accountant. Her moving on had come as more of a relief than a bother, proving to him once again that eventually all women leave.

Eva fidgeted in her chair. "So, will you do it?"

Adam stared at her. Not only wasn't Eva Burgess

backing down from her peculiar request, she was determined to see it through. He was hard-pressed not to instantly accept the assignment within an assignment.

"Just like that?" he asked, tugging at his tie. "Don't I even get some time to think about it?" ·

Eva pushed up from her chair and lifted her still-full mug of tea. "I don't have much time to give you. I'm on my way to Louisiana in two hours." She started for the door, then stopped. "I'd really appreciate it if you could do this for me, Adam. I know I haven't been exactly…warm toward you since you hired on, but I'm desperate. I wouldn't ask such a tremendous favor otherwise."

All at once the image of Eva Burgess stretched out on his sailboat became so clear it was almost a wet memory.

She cleared her throat. "I'll be in my office getting the Honeycutt account ready to take with me. Let me know what you decide."

Adam went on instant alert. *The Honeycutt account…*

EVA CLOSED ADAM'S office door, then leaned against it. She couldn't bring herself to believe what she had just done. For Pete's sake, she'd just asked a complete stranger to be her husband for the weekend. She swallowed hard. Sure, she and Adam worked at the same accounting firm. And aside from the awkward moment when he'd fumbled through a dinner invitation, he was polite, humble and attractive in a nerdy kind of way. But none of that changed that he was still a stranger.

She pushed away from the door and groaned. Not that his being a stranger mattered. There wasn't a chance in a thousand that Adam Gardner would agree to her plan. His horrified expression when she blurted out her proposal told her that.

She moved down the hall toward her own office. She had been stupid even to consider carrying out such a ruse. But when her mother had urged her to come, Eva had immediately agreed. If her mother thought she should be there, then her father's health must be at serious risk. Eva quickened her step, fear for her father's well-being spreading through her anew. The thought that she might never get the chance to put things right between them, to repair the rift that had always gaped between them, worried her all the more. Especially now. When the link between generations meant more to her than it ever had before.

Eva pressed her fingertips against her forehead. If only her mother hadn't insisted she bring her husband along. And if only she hadn't caved under Katina Mavros's loving but resourceful persuasiveness and agreed to that impossible request. Eva suspected that her mother's insistence grew as much out of concern for her and Bill's marriage as it did from her desire that son- and father-in-law finally meet. Ever since last week when Eva had inadvertently spilled some of the problems she and Bill were having, she'd regretted saying anything. If her mother only knew how very serious, and very final, those problems were.

The solution, of course, would have been to tell her mother the truth. But she hadn't had the guts then, and certainly not now, given her father's present state. And not when that truth was so new she had yet to completely accept it herself. After all, only a day had passed since she'd received her final divorce papers. She stumbled on the carpeting. How, exactly, did she explain to her father—sick or otherwise—that she was divorced when neither of her parents had ever met her husband?

A dull ache pounded a threatening rhythm at her temples. Crossing to her office, Eva put her cup on her desk then searched through the right-hand drawer for a couple of aspirin. She took a deep breath and halted her hands midway through working open the child-proof cap. Considering her own condition, she wasn't sure if she should be casually taking even aspirin. With a sigh she dropped the unopened bottle back into the drawer and slammed it shut, the rest of the reason she couldn't tell her father why she was divorced making her headache double in severity.

God, could things get much worse?

She dropped into her chair, reminding herself that yes, circumstances could be much worse.

Number one, she might be faced with going to Belle Rivage with her ex-husband. A man who had walked out on her without so much as a backward glance, taking with him the furniture and belongings they had accumulated during their one-year marriage. Then she'd have to deal with the prospect of concealing all the pain that still pulsed through her. Pain caused by his callous, piercing betrayal.

She rested her forehead in her hand, her thoughts making her hurt all over again.

She forced herself to concentrate on number two: Adam Gardner could agree to her outlandish proposal.

She lifted her head from her hand, envisioning the scenario. If Adam did accept her offer, she'd be faced with trying to fool her family into believing a man who was alternately awkward and inexplicably provocative whenever he was around her was her husband. She rested her fingers against her neck. No matter how attractive Adam might be if he lost the out-of-style glasses, and stopped putting gel on his hair, the idea of spending so much time around him somehow made her uneasy. She guessed it might be because of the way he'd looked in his office just now. Both shocked and appealing. Shocked, she had expected. Appealing was a different matter entirely.

She pushed the unwelcome thought away.

Whatever the outcome of this weekend, one thing rang perfectly clear. She might never bridge the gap between her and her father if she told him the truth now. Her father's Greek background and his passionate belief in traditional values would never allow him to see past her divorce. No matter that the friction between them had only been aggravated by her having married without his consent a year ago. Her latest failure would only reinforce his conviction that she'd been wrong to marry a man he had never met. And, given her current state, she wouldn't be surprised if he tried to marry her off to the first available, appropriate male. Appropriate in his eyes. A prison term in hers.

And that was the reason she chose Adam Gardner to play the role of her husband.

Eva smoothed a shaking hand over her hair. For a full hour after her mother's call she had mulled over what to do. And she'd decided that making her parents dislike her husband—or Adam in the role of her husband—*before* she shared the news, would make it much easier for them…and her.

She only wished she didn't feel so guilty. Not only for deceiving her family, but because if Adam accepted, she would be thrusting him into a situation where he would be placed so fully, so unflatteringly, on display.

Glancing at her wristwatch, Eva hauled her heavy attaché case onto her desktop. She opened it and stared at the envelope from her husband's lawyer sitting on top of a stack of files. Correction, her *ex-husband's* lawyer. She'd have to get used to saying that. Ex-husband. She winced. It was disheartening how two little letters

of the alphabet could change a family with promise
into a past relationship with failure written all over it.

Slipping the envelope off to the side, she pulled two
accordion files from her drawer and laid them inside
the attaché. She halted. She'd forgotten she wanted to
take the diskettes on the Honeycutt account. She
sighed, already having wished Norman Sheffert a
happy Labor Day when the next few days would likely
prove a virtual hell for her. Norman kept all the accounting diskettes in his office safe, for security reasons he said. Eva called it an inconvenience. Especially
since Norman was the only one who had access to the
safe. Not even the two senior partners, Gerry Logan or
Evan Brace, could get in without Norman's approval.
Though the fact didn't seem to bother either of them.
They were perfectly content to let Norman run the entire operation.

Eva got up from her chair and hurried down the hall
to where she hoped Norman's secretary, Alice Turley,
was still working. The humming computer and covered desk told her the peacock-like woman was
around somewhere.

Sighing, she stepped partway down the hall. "Alice?"

A sound from Norman's office caught her attention.
Eva stepped nearer. She knocked once, then opened
the door. Light from multiple sources illuminated the
interior but the office was empty. She stared at the ma-
hogany desk in the corner and stepped farther into the
room. *That's odd…what's the safe doing open?*

"Alice?" a male voice called out.

Eva jumped and turned to face Adam who stood in
the open doorway. "You startled me."

"Sorry," he said quietly. "I was going to ask Alice if
she'd seen you anywhere."

"I think the applicable question is have I seen Alice anywhere. To which I'd have to say no."

He glanced around the room. "I thought Sheffert left."

"He did." Eva shivered, then wrapped her arms around her waist.

A dark eyebrow lifted above the rim of Adam's glasses. An eyebrow that was silky and soft and perfectly shaped. "He left his office and safe open?"

Eva tugged her gaze away from his face, wondering why she always had the baffling urge to study him whenever he was near. "It's odd, considering how security-conscious Norman is. Not like him at all."

"I'll say."

Eva frowned. How would he know about Norman's behavior? He'd only been here three weeks.

Adam's eyebrow dropped and his intense expression melted away. Eva felt slightly relieved. For a moment there, she'd questioned bashful Adam Gardner's behavior.

"Maybe he was in such a hurry he forgot to lock up, that's all," he said, offering a shy smile and pushing up his glasses.

"Yes, that's probably it." The way his lips turned up at the sides gave him a wry appeal. Her gaze lingered on his mouth. "Anyway, what are the odds that on the same day Norman overlooks locking his safe, someone would be in here to steal the contents?"

"Good point."

The reason Adam might be looking for her suddenly dawned on Eva. A knot pulled tight in her stomach. Both at the thought that she might have to live up to her ruse, and that if she did, for the next day she would have to act as this man's *wife*. A man she felt both emotionally safe and unsafe around. Safe because his appearance made him seem like nothing more than geeky, brother material. Unsafe because the way he sometimes looked at her, like now, with that inexplicable gleam in his eyes, made her want to rub a hand over his nerdy exterior to learn what truly dwelled within.

"So, are you here to answer my proposal?" she said carefully, her palms growing damp.

"Yes, you could say that." He ran long and lean fingers down the length of his hideous tie then cleared his throat.

"And?" *Oh please, don't let him say no. No! Please don't let him say yes.*

His eyes locked with hers. She could swear by the subtle quirk of his eyebrows that he was teasing her. As if he knew exactly what he was doing by dragging out his answer. His gaze raked over her face and she battled the urge to pull her suit jacket closer as protection against...protection against what?

Finally, he said, "And...despite whatever misgivings I may have, I've decided it's in my best interest to help you out in your time of crisis."

A mixture of relief and uneasiness saturated her tense muscles. *He's doing it.*

"Best interest?" she repeated.

"You *are* my superior. I figure it couldn't hurt to have you owing me one come review time." He pushed up his glasses. "Besides, I've never been to New Orleans. Is it nice?"

Review time. Yes, she supposed she could put in a good word or two for him then. Her gaze dropped to his mouth. He'd already proved himself a competent accountant, so it wouldn't be too much of a hardship. He fingered his tie, apparently uncomfortable with her assessing gaze. She fought a small smile. Adam wasn't to blame if his social skills were a bit lacking. She wouldn't be surprised if he couldn't tell the difference between Chinese food and the northern version of Creole fare. But he would learn.

"Yes, New Orleans is very nice," she said, thinking the word didn't come near describing the sultry city. The image of Adam Gardner standing in the middle of decadent Bourbon Street held a certain appeal. She straightened slightly, finding that the thought more than attracted her, it stirred something fundamental within her. A mixture of curiosity and disquiet that left her wanting to expose him to the naughtier side of life, yet at the same time protect him from it. A reaction she didn't welcome even in passing. In fact, maybe this whole thing wasn't such a good idea after all.

"I guess we have a deal then," Adam said, extending his hand, nervously retracting it, then thrusting it out again.

She stared at his large hand, noticing the blunt ends of his fingers, the dark hair that dusted the back of his hand. She hesitantly gave it a brief shake. Her own palm was slick where his was remarkably warm and dry. The brief friction as skin met skin sent a trail of awareness up her arm. She quickly withdrew her hand.

"Good," she said, accepting that the ruse she had concocted was actually going to happen.

Adam wiped his palm on his slacks.

"I can't believe I almost forgot why I came in here." Eva turned away from him, then stepped to the open safe and crouched down. She searched for the needed diskettes, disappointed to find her hands trembling.

"What are you two doing in here?"

Eva started and watched two cases tip forward, spilling three-and-half-inch disks all over the carpet around her knees.

Alice-the-Hun, wearing one of her psychedelic skirts

with a fuchsia blazer, hurried into the room and fairly swooped down on Eva.

"Norman asked me to take over the Honeycutt account from Oliver. You know, to prepare for their review," Eva said to Sheffert's secretary, reaching down to collect the scattered disks. She shoved half of them back into the safe and nearly yelped when Alice snapped the safe door closed.

"I'll see to the rest," she said curtly.

Eva rose with hesitant help from Adam.

Alice turned. "All requests for disks come through me, you know that. And from what I know about Honeycutt's schedule, there's no reason for you to need those diskettes now. Their FTC review isn't for three months."

Eva faced her. "I thought I'd take a look at them this weekend—"

"No harm done, Alice," Adam said smoothly. "Why not just let Eva go ahead and get what she needs." He turned on a smile that made Eva blink. "Certainly there isn't a problem with that?"

"Problem?" Alice's hand fluttered to the costume-jewel pin at her throat. She looked at a spot behind them before her gaze hastened back to their faces. "Yes, there is a problem. While Eva may have been given the go-ahead on the Honeycutt account, I haven't yet been told."

Eva stared at her. Was Sheffert's fiftyish secretary attracted to Adam? She shifted her attention to the tall man next to her. She hadn't noticed exactly *how* tall Adam was until that moment. Usually when she saw him, he was sitting behind a desk or at a conference table. Now she noted that he towered over her five-feet-five-inch height in heels by more than half a foot.

She glanced behind her to see what had caught Alice's eye.

"There they are." On Sheffert's desk sat a small pile of diskettes Eva identified by their labels as belonging to the Honeycutt account. She crossed the room to pick them up. "Norman must have taken them out for me before he left."

She turned from the desk to find Alice standing obstinately in front of her. "To the contrary, Norman left the safe open so I could put the disks away."

"Look, Alice," Eva said, wondering what was with the woman, "Norman won't mind my checking the disks out. Now that Oliver is…no longer with the company, the account is mine and I'd like to familiarize myself with it. If it bothers you so much, why don't you check with Norman yourself?"

Alice's gaze again flicked to a spot over Eva's shoulder. "I think I'll do that."

"Good," Adam said. "Since we've reached an agreement of sorts, we'll be on our way then." His smile held a hint of charm, drawing Eva's gaze to the cleft in his chin. Little more than a dimple she had once thought added to his nerdiness, she now found it incredibly appealing. "Have a nice weekend, won't you, Alice?"

Adam wrapped his fingers around Eva's arm, helped her from between Alice and the desk, then steered her toward the door and out into the hall. His grip was oddly commanding. Eva was thankful for the slight change in his personality, if only for the fact that it got her out from under Alice's scrutiny.

He let her go the instant they stood in her office. Eva released a breath she hadn't been aware she was holding.

"Thanks," she said, brushing a strand of hair back from her face, unsure how she felt about Adam's casual, though self-assured touch.

"For what?"

She looked at him, searching for some sign that he'd noticed her reaction. He hadn't. *Good.* "For helping me out. I didn't know anyone could handle Alice."

Adam grimaced. "I wouldn't say I exactly handled her. I...I happen to like her, that's all."

Eva twisted her lips. If he was telling the truth, then he was the sole person in the place who *did* like the stern, flashy woman. "She obviously likes you, too, Adam."

She rounded her desk.

"Eva, do you mind if I ask you a question?"

She glanced at him. "Go ahead."

"How much of you asking me to play the role of your husband has to do with my being, well, a friend of mine says I'm a geek?"

Eva gave him a once-over, choosing her words carefully. Especially considering the curious thoughts she'd had about him just a short time ago. But now that there was a desk between them, and he no longer towered over her, she found it much easier to resist such thoughts. "Geek? Why, Adam, I don't think you're a geek."

Boy, she was going to pay for that whopper. She shrugged off any odd, lingering attraction to him, questioning her own faculties. God didn't make them any nerdier than Adam Gardner. Sure, he might be a little over six feet tall, and she guessed his hair was golden blond under all that gel he used. And she supposed his eyes were well-lashed and nicely shaped, and his grin the type that might attract attention with that yummy dimple. But Adam Gardner used none of these qualities to his advantage. Instead, they were lost behind his thick glasses, hidden under the hair gel and diminished by his nerdy, sometimes awkward movements and unpolished smiles.

He was the type of man her father would hate on sight.

She tugged her gaze away from him, reminding herself that was exactly the reason she'd chosen him. Still, it wouldn't do to insult the very person she needed to help her out of this jam.

"What would make you ask such a question?"

He shrugged his wide shoulders. "I don't know. I can't help wondering why you would ask me to do this for you." He pushed his glasses up so high Eva was certain his lashes brushed against the lenses when he blinked. Which was often. "Wait a minute. Does this situation require we sleep in the same room?"

Eva nearly choked. The concern was one she'd addressed immediately upon concocting her outlandish plan. "Um, yes, it does, Adam. But don't worry," she said quickly, resting her palms against the desk, afraid the prospect of sharing a room would scare him off. "My room at my parents' house has twin beds. Besides, our charade will only be for public purposes. I wouldn't expect you to, well, you know...."

"Perform in private?" he asked.

She stiffened and slowly lifted her hands from the desk. Where had that come from? She tensed from head to feet, acutely aware that within the next few hours she would be sharing a room with the man across from her. A man who was awkward and nerdy, yet still a man. A very tall man. With large hands. And the capacity to say things that surprised her...causing a peculiar twinge in her stomach and an inexplicable awareness to hum through her at the most unexpected, inconvenient times.

She pushed her words past her tight throat. "That's certainly one way to put it." She looked at her watch, disappointed to find her hand trembling again. "I have to get going so I can pack. What's your address? I'll pick you up in an hour."

2

WHATEVER HAPPENED this weekend, the assignment ended here.

Adam stood at the curb in front of his West Edison condo, his carryall and briefcase resting at his wing-tip-clad feet. Five minutes ago, he'd had a heated discussion with John Weckworth, who thought it a bad idea for him to go through with Eva Burgess's bizarre request.

"What if she's in cahoots with Sheffert?" Weckworth had asked. "What if she's working with him and they've discovered you're not who you're supposed to be?"

What if, indeed.

Adam glanced at his watch, then rubbed his freshly shaven chin. It would be wise to keep Weckworth's words in mind. Especially given the peculiar circumstances surrounding Oliver Pinney's disappearance.

Weckworth's questioning of Pinney a month ago had been nothing but an ordinary inquiry. The firm had been in the middle of an open FBI audit and Pinney was in charge of those clients with shady connections to organized crime.

But there had been nothing ordinary about Oliver Pinney's behavior during the meeting. A weakness a pro like Weckworth knew exactly how to exploit. Two hours after the interview began, Pinney had cracked.

"Sheffert will have me filed away permanently," the high-strung junior accountant had told Weckworth.

"He didn't think I knew what he was doing. What he was having me do." Beads of sweat had popped from every pore of Pinney's pinched face. "He has one of the most sophisticated tax evasion and money laundering operations on the East Coast. It doesn't matter where the money comes from, give it to him and he'll have it squeaky clean and tucked neatly away in no time."

Then Oliver Pinney, the sole witness they had—the only evidence they had—had disappeared. The open audit was immediately closed without prejudice and Adam was sent in undercover.

And now he was embarking on a weekend foray with a woman he barely knew. A woman he hoped held the key to breaking this investigation wide open.

This little stint should be a piece of cake, nothing like other roles he'd played as a midwestern mercenary with a third-grade education and membership in every subversive group this side of the Mississippi. Still, the prospect of playing a paranoid revolutionary was preferable to acting as though he were a member of someone's family. He'd be the first to admit that having no family of his own had made him a prime candidate for the FBI. He had no weak spots, no vulnerable wife, children, parents or siblings to put at risk.

That fact also ill equipped him for the job ahead.

Adam rolled his bunched shoulders. He'd go along with Eva's plan, while working on his own agenda. His purpose—to get her to reveal, directly or indirectly, what her boss was up to. And if she was involved in Sheffert's scheme? The thought bothered him. Well, if she was involved, it wouldn't be the first time a woman had disappointed him.

"Adam?" a familiar voice said. If only it were the familiar voice he expected. He bit back a curse.

So much for his background not interfering with his job.

He was going to have to be more careful from here on out.

Stiffly, he turned to face his last indulgence. "What are you doing here, Julia?" he asked, glancing up the street. It was empty, though he doubted it would be for long. "I didn't expect you. You should have called." It wouldn't do for Eva to see him talking to the red-haired, self-proclaimed bombshell. Especially since Julia had decked herself out for the occasion. He cringed at her red leggings and gold lamé top.

She shrugged off his suggestion. "I really didn't think a phone call was necessary." She clutched an empty paper bag in her hands. "I'm just stopping by to pick up my things."

Adam was almost relieved. Almost. At least Julia didn't harbor any illusions about them picking up where they'd left off.

In any case, he didn't have the time to deal with her now. Especially since he'd accidentally washed a couple items of clothing she'd left behind with his. A few pieces clearly marked Dry-Clean Only that now sat in a faded, shrunken mess in a small box in the bedroom closet.

Julia gave him the once-over. "You remind me of a nerd I went to high school with." She grinned and swung her hair over a freckled shoulder. "I hope I didn't do that to you."

Adam nearly chuckled. "I really wish I could help you out, Julia, but I'm just about to leave on a business trip."

"That's okay. Just give me the key. I'll lock up when I'm done." She waggled her fingers.

Adam weighed his options: either deny Julia and risk having Eva see her and blow his cover, or hand over his keys and hope Julia would understand when she found her ruined clothes.

Damn.

A block up, a black Mercedes turned onto the street. He had no doubt it was Eva. Not the way his luck was running. In fact, he wouldn't be the least bit surprised if the gray clouds in the dark sky opened up and drenched him.

He handed over his apartment key.

"Just leave the place the way you found it, okay? And give the key to my next-door neighbor when you're done," he grumbled, watching Julia sashay toward the apartment door.

Just let me get out of here without incident.

Eva pulled up to the curb. A loud click told him she had unlocked the doors. He stowed his things in the back seat. A seat burdened with her attaché, a small tote and a pair of sandals, while clothes hung from a clip above a door window.

Almost there.

He opened the passenger's door just as he heard the unmistakable sound of an apartment window sliding open. An object whizzed past his ear then landed with a thud behind him.

"What did you do to my things?" Julia cried from the second-story window. "Do you know how much those clothes *cost?* You're going to reimburse me every stinking penny, you rat!"

Dodging what looked like one of his best Italian shoes, Adam cursed. He'd hoped he'd have more time before Julia found the box. Wishful thinking.

It began to sprinkle.

He quickly got into the car.

"Don't you *dare* go anywhere, you bastard!" Julia cried, sending a handful of clothing sailing through the air.

Adam said hello to Eva then slammed the door. On second thought, maybe it wasn't such a good idea to give Julia free rein over his apartment. Lord knew what he'd find when he got back from Louisiana.

He pushed his glasses up, watching a pair of red silk boxers float down to land on the windshield...directly in front of Eva's shocked face.

Adam opened the window and snatched the boxers from view. He stuffed the scrap of material into his pocket. Definitely not something a repressed accountant was sure to own.

Eva leaned toward the windshield, flinching when another handful of clothes sailed through the air. "Who's that?"

"Who's who?" Adam asked.

Eva stared at him.

"Oh, her. That's my...neighbor." *Neighbor. Yeah, right. Where had he come up with that one?* "She's upset because her husband stayed at my place last night after an argument."

"Then those aren't your things?"

"What? The clothes? No, they're her husband's."

Eva's gaze dropped to the silk spilling from his pocket.

"He's going to be surprised when he gets home, huh?" He shoved the boxers farther into his pants pocket. "Nice car. Do they pay you that well at the firm?" The question was meant to distract. He knew her yearly salary down to the last dollar. And she could easily afford the car.

She didn't rise to the bait.

"I was afraid you weren't going to show," he said, trying again.

Finally, Eva's gaze moved from his pocket to his face. "I was afraid I wasn't going to show, either," she said slowly, then shifted the car into Drive. "You changed."

It took a moment for Adam to realize she meant he'd

changed his clothes. She slowly zigzagged through the garments littering the street, then made a turn at the first corner. Adam relaxed slightly. He glanced down at the plain brown slacks and short-sleeved white shirt he had on, nearly not recognizing himself.

"Yes, I thought it would be more comfortable for the drive."

The farther away from the condo and the vengeful Julia they moved, the more in control Adam felt.

"Drive?" Eva blinked at him. "We're not driving. We're flying. Didn't I tell you?"

He stared at her light green suit. She hadn't changed, but somehow managed to look as fresh as she had that morning. A sharp contrast to the skintight, racy clothes Julia always wore.

Adam pushed up his glasses, hiding his frown. He'd already worked out that an airplane was out of the question. Not a good idea to let Eva see him checking his pistol at the airport. "No, you didn't tell me. If you had, I would have told you I can't fly."

The suspicion in her eyes deepened. "I don't understand."

"I suffer from a severe case of acrophobia." Adam cleared his throat. "I'm sorry, I guess I should have told you, you know, earlier when you asked me to go."

Eva touched her fingertips to her forehead. "Yes, you should have."

Adam examined the situation carefully. Better to act contrite. "If it's too much of an inconvenience, you could take me back home."

Her worried expression told him she was considering it. Which didn't work into his plans at all.

"I'll share responsibility for the driving, if you want," he said. "We could reach Louisiana by early tomorrow afternoon."

Eva flicked on her turn signal and pulled into a gas

station. He feared she was going to turn around, until she parked next to a pump. She told the attendant to fill the tank.

Adam watched her grimace. "I guess we're driving then, aren't we?"

He tried his best to look chagrined.

"Don't worry about it," she said. "We need to brief you on what my parents know about my husband, anyway. This will just give us a little more time to do it."

"Ex-husband."

He watched her wince. "Somehow I don't think I should get used to using that term. At least not this weekend, if you know what I mean. It could cause some problems should I accidentally introduce you as my ex." She toyed with the clip holding her hair firmly in place. "It also would negate the entire reason I'm taking you with me."

He nodded and, as an afterthought, secured his seat belt. That's what geek Adam would have done the instant he got into the car. He suppressed the urge to sink into the soft leather seat. No matter how much he wished he and Eva Burgess were heading for a weekend rendezvous that included little more than that naughty bikini he kept seeing her in, he was still on assignment. And that meant staying in character.

He cursed silently. Figures. He was with the first woman who had looks and an attractive mind and he had to act like the dork from hell. He lay his head against the headrest. How was he ever going to get close enough to break through her icy reserve this way?

Silence reigned after she paid the attendant then drove toward Interstate 95. Rain pelted the windshield and she switched on the wipers, the rhythmic sound enticingly intimate as he breathed in the sophisticated scent radiating from her skin.

He leaned closer to her, stopping a couple inches away from her neck. "What's the perfume you're wearing?"

"What?"

Adam slowly lifted his gaze from the alluring curve of her neck. "Your perfume. What's the name of it?"

She turned to stare at him. Her eyes widened fractionally, apparently in response to finding him so close. "I…I, uh, really don't see where that's any concern of yours, Adam. I thought I made it clear that…that I—"

"That you have no interest in getting involved with anyone," he finished for her. "I know." He forced himself to draw back. It was enough for now to know he affected her with his nearness. "I'm not asking for personal reasons. Isn't the name of your perfume something your husband would know?"

"Oh."

Adam wished it were lighter so he could make out the blush that almost surely colored her creamy skin.

"Normally, yes, I suppose it is something a husband would know," she said carefully. "It's Poison."

He fastened his gaze on the rain-drenched road before them. Poison. Her choice of perfumes was both fitting and frustrating. Fitting in the way that if someone got too close, she wouldn't hesitate to use the verbal equivalent of venom to get rid of them. Frustrating because the scent was provocative and sensual, two descriptions he would have thought junior partner Eva Burgess would have avoided at all costs.

He cleared his throat. "You said that as though your husband wasn't exactly…normal."

With one hand, Eva tried to take off her right earring, softly cursing when she dropped a portion of it.

"About my ex...well, he wasn't institution material, if that's what you mean. Then again, since I don't have anyone to compare him with, I can't exactly say whether Bill was a normal husband or not."

Adam scrambled to help her find the piece of her earring, figuring it was just the thing Adam-the-geek would do. His hand brushed the back of hers. She instantly pulled away.

"Sorry," he said quietly.

Her skin was as he had imagined it would be: soft. Almost wickedly so. That didn't surprise him. What did surprise him was its warmth. He'd imagined Eva's chilly disposition would stretch to her skin. The contrast intrigued him, as well as made him wary. Who would have guessed nippy, professional Eva Burgess's skin would be hot to the touch? Until now, he had imagined the many ways he could thaw her. He swallowed hard, realizing it might not be a matter of thawing her at all, but instead finding the perfect way to coax out her inner fire. To let it burn out of control and consume them both.

Eva Burgess's husband *was* institution material for leaving her.

Adam shifted, suddenly uneasy in the comfortable seat. He reminded himself he knew next to nothing about the woman sitting beside him. And despite his brief forays into a fantasy world that made his assignment a little less dull, this *was* an assignment. He'd be better off if he kept that clearly in mind. A mutual...coming together with Eva was agreeable, but beyond that he had no room in his plans—personal or professional—for a serious relationship. Certainly not one where the word *spouse* was included.

"So is that to be my name for the weekend? Bill?" he asked, clearing his throat. He sought and found the small gold backing in the carpet. He picked it up. "Here."

Without looking at him, she held out her hand, palm up. "Yes. My husband's…ex-husband's name is William Burgess. Bill to his friends."

Adam couldn't resist brushing his fingertips against the sensitive skin of her palm. He could have sworn she shivered as she closed her fingers around the backing and drew her hand away.

"Does he have many?" he asked. "Friends, I mean?"

The headlights of an oncoming car illuminated her strained features. "I once thought I was one. His best, if you want the truth. Now, well, I guess I was wrong." Eva said the last sentence so quietly, Adam wondered if he'd heard it at all.

She tightened her hands on the steering wheel. "Anyway, yes, Bill has many friends. Comes with the job, he told me." She glanced in Adam's direction. "He's a broker."

"A stockbroker?" He'd focused his investigative skills on a few brokers in the past. At least he'd know how to emulate one.

"Yes. He commuted from Edison to New York."

The rain started coming down in thick sheets and Eva switched on the brights. Adam stared out at the soggy onslaught. So his identity was to be Bill Burgess, stockbroker from New York, husband to Eva Burgess, who wore Poison. What was it like to be married to Eva? Not the junior partner of an accounting firm, but the woman? Adam found her face pale and tight as she concentrated on driving in the late-summer storm.

"Do you want me to take over?" he asked as she slowed.

She shook her head. "No, I'm okay. But I don't think I'm going to be very good company for a while. At least not until we get out of this storm." She gestured toward his door. "The seat tilts back. Why don't you try to get some sleep? We'll trade spots sometime around three."

Three. As in 3:00 a.m. Adam frowned. It had been a long time since he'd taken a road trip. He toyed with the buttons on his door panel until he got his chair where he wanted it. Then he lay back at a stiff angle, in a way consistent with his role. He noticed Eva's small, secret smile as she stole a glance at him.

Adam bit back a curse. Somehow this wasn't exactly how he'd imagined their first date.

FOUR AND A HALF HOURS later, the car slowed. Through narrowed lids, Adam watched Eva pull onto the shoulder of the Virginia highway. She flicked on the hazards and shoved open her door, racing through the steady rain toward the weeds at the side of the road. Adam sat up and watched her double over, her silhouette little more than a blur through the torrential downpour. Frowning, he snapped open the glove compartment. He took out a box of tissues, then sifted through the rest of the items. A brush, a couple of toll stubs and parking permits.

Eva climbed back into the car. Adam shut the compartment then handed her a wad of tissues.

"Looks like you and cars get along about as well as me and planes," he murmured.

If she'd been pale earlier, now she was downright white. The rain had loosened strands of hair from her French twist and they hung in wet silken threads around her damp face. She pushed them back. It was something Adam found himself wanting to do.

Her gaze darted to the rearview mirror as she slammed her door shut. "I guess the stress of all that's happened today just caught up with me."

He began to hand her fresh tissues, then changed his

mind and gently eased the box into her shaking hands. Why did he have the unsettling feeling stress wasn't behind Eva's quick trip to the side of the road?

"I saw a sign indicating a rest area coming up," he said. "Why don't you let me drive there and we'll get something to settle your stomach?"

She blinked at him. "I thought you were sleeping."

"No. I can't sleep around strangers. I'm too afraid I'll do something embarrassing, like get caught drooling or something." He reached for the door handle, relieved when she didn't try to stop him. By the time he rounded the driver's side, he was soaked. He cleaned off his rain-speckled glasses, then adjusted the seat and started off again.

Within minutes, he was waiting in the atrium outside the ladies' room for Eva to come out. It was 1:00 a.m. and the restaurants the rest area boasted were closed. Plate-glass windows faced the parking area and he stared through the rain at where another car pulled up.

"Sorry I took so long," Eva said, rejoining him. "Let's go."

"Whoa." Adam lay a hand against her arm. "I think your body could do with a little rest. Why don't we get some coffee or something?" he said, gesturing at a row of vending machines.

"Coffee?"

Adam's gaze swept her face, finding the color had returned to her cheeks, a reassuring sign even if her eyes were a little too bright. She'd released her hair from its usual restraints. It surprised him with its silken length, stretching down her back in dark, thick tangles. He'd pegged her as the conservative type who wouldn't let her hair grow past her shoulders.

First the heat of her skin...now the length of her hair. So far he was zero for two on the assumptions he'd made about Eva Burgess. Zero for three if you counted her bizarre request that he play her husband for the weekend.

"I suppose I could do with a little decaf," she said softly.

She dug in her purse for change, but he slid his own coins into the metal slot and gestured for her to make her selection.

"Thanks." She poked the buttons for decaf, no cream, no sugar.

Her cup landed sideways in the slot, the coffee streaming off the side in a wide arc that nearly hit her green skirt.

"Figures," Eva murmured.

"Here, let me try," Adam said, pushing up his glasses. "Machines and I speak the same language."

Moments later, he handed her a fresh, intact cup, and she thanked him again.

He made his selection. Extra strong with plenty of sugar and cream. The cup slid down...sideways. The coffee sprayed the knees of his brown slacks. Eva laughed.

"Looks like a breakdown in communication," she said. "Here, why don't we just share mine? I can't drink it all, anyway. I mean, if you don't mind it without sugar and cream."

He glanced at her, the prospect of sharing something as innocuous as a cup of coffee with Eva striking him as somehow intimate. He finished mopping his pants with paper towels and motioned to a wood-backed bench near the doors. For long moments they sat there staring at the rain. She took a sip of the coffee, then handed it to him.

He purposely hesitated. Would a nerd so easily drink from the same cup as a stranger? "Are you sure whatever you got isn't contagious?"

She smiled softly. "Believe me, what I have, you can't catch." She flicked a damp strand of hair over her shoulder. "Sorry about that. I usually don't get carsick."

He eyed her carefully, finding her nearly as nervous as she'd been in his office that afternoon. She smoothed out her skirt repeatedly and kept crossing and uncrossing those marvelous legs of hers.

"Has it been a while since you've visited your parents?" he asked.

"A little over a year." Her gaze fastened on his mouth, then skittered away. "I usually get back more often, but this year's been rough." Her expression darkened, then she looked up. "I mean, it's been especially hectic at the office."

"Oh?" Adam doubted work was what had been on her mind. But work was exactly what he wanted to talk about. "It's been busy?"

"Not so much busy," she said, taking the cup back. "It's been more or less problems with personnel." She gestured toward him. "Take the guy you replaced."

"Oliver Pinney?"

A frown drew her feathery eyebrows together. "Yes. About a month ago during an audit, he just…disappeared." She looked away. "Well, not exactly disappeared without a trace, really. He left a typed resignation that was effective immediately." She looked down at her wet shoes. "I don't know, maybe it wouldn't strike me as being so odd, except shortly before he left, he'd been acting…I guess *anxious* is the word I'm looking for."

"How so?"

Whatever lipstick she'd had on earlier was gone. Adam found the natural color almost unbearably appealing. The two, tiny peaks at the top of her upper lip were perfectly defined, her lower lip a little fuller, her teeth white and smooth.

She took a small sip of coffee, apparently aware of his attention as she offered a shaky smile.

"I don't know, really. Whenever I talked to him, it was as though he really didn't hear me. I can't count the times I had to repeat myself." She skimmed her manicured, clear-polished nails against the length of the paper cup. "Word has it he and Norman had a falling-out last February, so maybe that was the cause of his anxiety."

Adam had caught wind of the rumor himself. But aside from raised voices coming from inside Norman Sheffert's office, no one had any idea what the disagreement was about. Given Pinney's subsequent questioning by Weckworth, Adam didn't have to wonder about the cause. He knew. Pinney had caught on to Sheffert's illegal dealings and must have confronted his boss with them.

"How long have you been at the firm?" Adam asked, though he already knew the answer.

"Six years." Eva raked her thick, glossy hair back from her face. "I came in as an intern after graduating from Rutgers and have been there ever since."

He was right. She had been away from Louisiana for a while.

"You and Sheffert get along well?"

Her eyes narrowed. Adam warned himself against sounding too un-geeklike. Especially so soon after the Julia episode. He pushed up his glasses for good measure. It seemed to do the trick.

"Yes, I suppose you could say Norman and I get along okay."

He cleared his throat and held out his hand for the cup. She gave it to him. "What about Norman and Oliver? Did they have a good work relationship? I mean, before the argument?"

She shrugged her slender shoulders and unbuttoned her blazer. "I guess. I never paid much attention." She opened her jacket. "Why all the questions?"

Adam managed a shrug. "Just curious."

Silently, he cursed. The sight of her white blouse plastered against what appeared to be a very lacy bra threatened to wipe all thought from his mind. All thought, that is, except how he'd like to explore the supple curve of her breasts. To draw the tips into his mouth and watch her melt with pleasure.

He caught the curious shadow in her eyes and decided now wasn't the time to pursue any more questions...or the other thoughts he had in mind. He'd have to earn her trust first. He sipped the coffee, looking out the window. Why did he have the sinking feeling that getting Eva to trust him wasn't going to be easy?

"Who's that?"

Adam jerked to find her staring out the window. "Who's who?"

"That man looking in my car."

Adam thrust the cup at her and leaped from the seat. Through the pouring rain, he vaguely made out a figure bending near the driver's side of the Mercedes.

"Did you lock the car?"

He had his answer when the man opened the door.

Adam cursed under his breath and rushed toward the double glass doors. He snatched off his glasses and bolted into the rain, Eva on his heels, as he thundered toward the car and the guy rummaging around inside. Damn, what did he think he was doing? He couldn't act the renegade when the most exercise Eva would expect from him were trips between his desk and the coffee machine. If he yanked the man out by the collar and interrogated him, it would surely make Eva more suspicious than ever.

The would-be thief spotted him, climbed from the car and ran in the opposite direction. While Adam could probably catch him, doing so was not a good idea.

Thinking fast, Adam feigned a stumble on the slick pavement. Eva slammed into his backside. He instantly turned to steady her, and she grabbed on to his arms to balance him. The quick movements put her lush body flat against the length of his. Her full, firm breasts pressed against his chest, her hips rested flush against his. She gave a small gasp that induced a similar arousing reaction in him. The fantasies he'd been entertaining about her all day surged back tenfold. Eva Burgess firmly crowded against him and the ineffectual way she tried to free herself did unwelcome, interesting things to his libido.

Adam's gaze dropped to her damp, berry-colored lips to find them slightly, enticingly parted. He groaned, filled with an incredible urge to kiss her. To sample the taste of that generous mouth. To see how her own unique flavor mingled with the wetness of the rain. He slowly inched his lips nearer to hers...then drew to a stop. *Where were his glasses?*

Eva went completely still, staring at him. Shock colored her appealing features as her gaze probed him from forehead to chin, lingering on his mouth mere inches away from hers. Her fingers tightened on his upper arms, as if exploring the muscles concealed beneath his shapeless shirt.

Oh, hell, I should have just gone for the guy and taken my chances, Adam thought. Better than having Eva figure out he wasn't the man he pretended because he'd kissed her. Even if it meant missing out on the taste of her lips.

"I'm so sorry," he said in a tight, geeklike manner, thrusting her away from him. "I've never been so embarrassed."

The move wiped the alert expression right off her face.

The thief was running toward the other side of the lot, a bright yellow rain slicker with a hood concealing his features. He looked about as experienced as a ten-year-old. Adam grimaced. He'd nearly blown his cover over some moron probably looking for change for the coffee machine.

"Are you all right?" Eva asked, straightening her jacket.

Adam kept his face averted.

"Fine…I'm fine," he said, watching a late-model Ford race from the far end of the lot and onto the interstate. Damn.

"You broke your glasses."

Adam looked to where he had dropped his eyeglasses. He picked them up to find an earpiece had snapped away cleanly.

"What did you think you were doing, running after him like that?" Eva asked, the beam of a streetlight bathing her in yellow.

Adam wanted to grin. What a picture they made. The two of them, drenched to the skin, Eva lecturing him.

She blinked at him, a frown on her alluring face. "You do have an extra pair of glasses, don't you?"

"No…I didn't think to bring them with me."

He followed her to the Mercedes.

"Did he take anything?" he asked, glancing around the dark interior.

Eva flicked on the dome light and shifted to look in the back seat.

"I can't be sure, but I don't think so."

Her attaché sat cockeyed on the seat, but was still closed, and his overnight bag had been opened, but was otherwise still intact.

That was no traveler looking for small change.

Adam stared in the direction the dark-colored Ford had gone. He'd like to have had a little one-on-one with the driver about what he'd been after. Adam's gut instincts told him the guy had been more than a simple thief.

"I think we should report it to the highway patrol," he said quietly.

She thought about it, looking first at the digital clock on the dash then out into the rain. "What's the point? It doesn't look like anything's missing. Besides, since we're driving, we're already way behind the schedule I gave my mother."

She switched off the overhead light and he squinted at her. In his goal to get her to trust him, he would have to demonstrate his trust in her and her judgment. That meant letting the Ford get away.

Eva seemed nervous. Which seemed right, considering she'd just had her car broken into. But somehow Adam didn't think that's what caused the wrinkle between her dark, soft eyebrows. Was it the prospect of talking to her mother? If so, why? Because her father was ill? Or did Eva Burgess know how to deal with everyone except her parents?

Interesting thought.

Not that he had firsthand experience with child-parent relationships. Raised by a foster family—who'd had their hands full with eight other parentless children—Adam had more or less charted his own, solitary course. What did it feel like to have family obligations? He didn't know, but judging by Eva's anxiety, he guessed it wasn't all peaches and cream.

He grimaced.

"What's the matter?" Eva asked quietly.

"Matter? Why would anything be the matter?"

"You frowned just now. Are you sure not going to the highway patrol is all right with you?"

"I'm positive. I've caused enough trouble by making us drive down, Eva. I don't want to be responsible for any more."

She reached out and laid her hand on his forearm, sparking all sorts of emotions that had nothing to do with naughty string bikinis or boats. "You haven't caused any trouble, Adam." She increased the pressure of her fingers against his skin. Again he was struck by the heat she radiated. "Everything considered, I think you're doing wonderfully." Her smile was sweet, reminding him he hadn't even noticed that the coffee they'd shared in the rest shelter had been black. "You're in a situation you didn't ask to be stuck in."

God, he was really coming to hate this geek stuff. "I'd offer to drive, but…"

"Oh, God, your glasses," she said quickly. "I'm sorry about that."

"Why? You didn't break them. I did."

"Yes, but if I had locked the car that guy wouldn't have gotten inside, and you would never have run after him." She frowned. "Why *did* you run after him, anyway?"

There it was. The suspicion he'd dreaded. Good thing he hadn't turned the thief into a hood ornament. He was pretty sure that little move would have put him on the first bus home. "Instinct, I guess. I don't have any idea what I would have done if I'd caught up with him."

She stared at him for a long moment, then smiled. "Thanks for the gesture, anyway. It's been a long time since someone did something brave on my behalf. I'd forgotten what it felt like."

He raked his hair into place and squinted, pretending he was lost without his glasses, though his vision was twenty-twenty. His accuracy at the firing range proved that. "Yes, I'd say almost falling flat on my butt qualifies me for hero status."

Her laugh rang low and enchanting as she backed the car out of the parking spot. "At least you tried. A lot of men I know wouldn't have done more than yell out, 'Hey you!' and expect the guy to freeze in his tracks."

His gaze roamed over her smiling face, then fastened on her wistful green eyes. "Are we talking about your husband again?"

Her smile vanished and everything about her tensed.

"*Ex*-husband," she said as she pulled back into the light highway traffic. "Maybe we can stop at one of those one-hour glasses places in the morning."

The pain in her eyes at the mention of her ex struck him in a way he was unprepared for. She looked abandoned. Alone. A long-buried part of Adam responded. He couldn't resist touching her hand where it lay against the steering wheel, no matter how unaccountably bold the action was.

"I shouldn't have brought him up," he said quietly.

She stared at where his hand lay against hers. Her throat contracted as she swallowed and he felt an answering twinge low in his stomach. Surprisingly, she didn't try to shake off his hand. In fact, she almost seemed to welcome the gesture.

"No problem," she said softly. "That's the reason you're on this trip anyway, right?"

He reluctantly removed his hand from hers. "Right."

3

THE FOLLOWING AFTERNOON Eva rushed around the rest-area ladies' room, a few minutes and a couple miles separating her from a family reunion that included her husband. Correction, a reunion that included the man acting as her husband.

Groaning, she gathered her cosmetics from where she had scattered them across the counter and shoved them into her overnight bag. A woman stepped next to her. Eva stared at her wristwatch. God, was it really four-thirty in the afternoon already? She wiped a smudge of lipstick from the corner of her mouth, trying not to notice the exhausted circles under her eyes from having been on the road for the past twenty hours straight.

She drew in a deep breath and prayed she could pull this off.

She emerged from the exterior door and a thick wave of heat crashed over her. She always forgot how swelteringly hot it got down here. She glanced toward the car to find Adam leaning against the front grille. The day was overcast and hazy, but there was no evidence of the deluge that had plagued them almost the entire trip down. Adam's face was drawn into stern lines as he watched the cars driving in and out of the parking area.

"Adam?" Eva asked.

He snapped instantly to attention. "Hi. Are you ready?"

Eva felt a pang of amusement. Somewhere in Tennessee he'd emerged from a service station with his glasses taped back together with gray duct tape. Gray duct tape, for God's sake. Did every nerd on earth know where to get a supply? Her anxiety momentarily forgotten, she watched him wipe the spot on the car he'd leaned against and told herself this ruse was going to work. Actually, it was going to go better than she hoped. There wasn't a chance her brash, hard-as-nails father would get along with the unassertive man before her. She could see it now: her father demanding she get rid of him, her refusing, then telling him after she returned to Jersey that she was getting divorced.

Eva worried her bottom lip. That's if she had the time to pull off such a plan. It depended on how sick her father was.

She rounded the car and popped open the trunk, stuffing her things inside.

"Eva, I...I like your dress."

She swiveled to find Adam standing directly behind her. She was struck again by how very tall he was and how very...wide. He smiled and the dimple in his chin winked at her. She was filled with a momentary desire to slip the tip of her finger into that cleft, then run that fingertip along the edge of his jawline, tracing a path down to his smooth-skinned neck....

Instead she cleared her throat and glanced down at the peasant-style dress she wore.

"Yes, well, it's not exactly office attire, but it's what my parents would expect me to wear." *What her father would want her to wear.* She slammed the trunk closed along with her runaway thoughts. "Speaking of my parents, we're late."

Adam wrapped his fingers around hers, the burst of heat his touch caused making the day seem cool in comparison. "Here, why don't you let me drive the rest of the way."

He pried the keys from her fingers. "All right."

She stared at him a moment. She didn't know what it was, but there was something about Adam that didn't add up. Just when she thought she had him figured out, he did something that threw her, something that didn't seem in character with the nerdy, shy guy she was coming to like. Something that set off warning bells in her head and caused awareness to curl through her.

"Are you ready?" he asked. "I don't know about you, but I'm so nervous that if we don't do this quick, I'll be tempted to call off the whole deal and go back to New Jersey."

She grinned. She was being ridiculous, of course. Her occasional reactions to Adam as a man were little more than hormones run amok. Adam was exactly what he appeared to be: a nice guy who posed no emotional threat to her whatsoever. More brother than lover material.

"You're right. Let's get this over with," she said, heading for the driver's side.

Adam caught her wrist. "You're over there."

"Oh. That's right."

They climbed into the car and Adam started the engine.

"Should we stop somewhere for a quick bite first?" Adam backed the car up.

"Bite?" Eva shuddered, the mere mention of food sending her stomach hurtling into her throat. She'd had a difficult time forcing down plain toast and tea earlier that morning.

"Aren't you hungry? I haven't seen you eat a whole heck of a lot since we got under way last night."

"No, I'm not." She shoved her hair back from her

face, wishing she'd had time to do something with it. "Anyway, I'm sure Yaya—that's my grandmother—will have something for us at the house. Whether we're hungry or not."

Adam slid a glance her way. "Ah, I see. You and the car still aren't getting along very well."

"The car and I are getting along just fine, thank you. Besides, I don't think car sickness is exactly what I suffered from last night. I might have a twenty-four-hour stomach flu or something."

Liar. Eva shrugged off the uneasiness clinging to her.

"I like your hair down."

She jerked to stare at him. "What?"

"I said I like your hair down. You always wear it up at work. It looks nice down, loose."

His gaze seemed oddly provocative.

"Thanks." She threaded her fingers through the soft strands. "Now, this is the last chance we have to get the details about my ex down for my family."

"Right."

"Tell me what you've got so far."

Adam tugged at his collar. "You mean aside from the fact that he's an idiot for having left you?"

Eva was unsure how to take his comment. "We're talking about the time before he left."

"Right," he said again. "Well, then, my name is William Burgess, Bill to my friends. I'm a stockbroker who commutes from my home in Edison, New Jersey, to New York." He glanced at her. "Do I take the bus or drive?"

"Drive."

"Isn't that expensive?" he asked.

Yes, it was expensive, considering the parking costs in Manhattan. Bill's insistence on driving his new BMW to work had been the source of plenty of arguments. Though she realized it wasn't the car but the man and his values she objected to.

"That doesn't matter. Actually, the question is moot, because my parents wouldn't know whether he drove or not."

His frown was apparent. "What *do* they know about him?"

"Not much, other than I worked on one of Bill's accounts, we became friends, then were married last year by a judge."

"You were friends first?"

Eva waved, uneasy with her slip. She didn't like admitting that she'd made the grave error of thinking that since she and Bill had gotten along so well, theirs would be a worry-free union. A comfortable one. A stable one. *An easy-to-walk-away-from one.*

"Yes, but just tell them we dated. They only spoke once for a few minutes on the phone, but I doubt they'd remember the sound of Bill's voice. Anyway, you don't have to worry about emulating Bill exactly. I have something else in mind."

He was looking in the rearview mirror. "What about your family? Shouldn't I know something about them?"

"Turn here," she said quickly, realizing they were near her family home. She searched for signs of change in the tall, pale-wooded cypresses and Spanish moss–blanketed live oaks that pressed in on the narrow two-lane road. There was none. It wasn't the lush green landscape that had changed. She had.

"About my father...he's, uh, from Greece. Immigrated here when he was a teenager. He'll lapse into Greek sometimes, but don't worry about it. He doesn't do it to be rude." Which wasn't exactly true, but Adam didn't have to know that.

He quirked an eyebrow, raising it above the rim of his glasses. "Your mother?"

"She's Greek-American, born here. Yaya is her mother."

"I see."

"My father has a seafood company, Mavros Seafood. Oysters, mostly, but he does harvest some crabs and crawfish. I have a brother, Pete, and a horde of other relatives. Don't worry, you probably won't see them. Not if my father is as sick as I think he is."

She directed him to turn again. "It's the last house on the lane," she said, drawing a deep breath.

"One more thing, Eva," Adam said. "Is there any special way you want me to act? What I mean is, did Bill do anything like…" His gaze shifted away. "Like hold your hand, or something, when you were around people.…"

Eva managed a smile. "No. I just want you to act like yourself, Adam. That should work out fine."

ADAM CLIMBED from the car, looking at the road they had turned off of. Ever since the incident at the rest area, he'd been keeping an eye out for the Ford, unable to shake the feeling that something more than petty theft had been going on back there. He frowned. Unfortunately, it appeared half the population owned dark-colored Fords.

He turned toward the sprawling villa-like structure before him. His gaze shifted from the red-tiled roof, the cool, white stucco walls, curved window arches and the sweeping front porch complete with columns. The lush yard was dotted with cypress trees and a huge, dripping willow with a swing hanging from one of the branches. Adam found his surroundings an interesting mix of the Mediterranean and the tropics smack-dab in the middle of the bayous of Louisiana. He closed the car door, shifting his gaze to Eva who stood smoothing the skirt of her dress.

"Are you okay?" he asked, rounding the car. He touched her forearm, his fingers fitting nicely around the slender limb.

Her eyes held a faraway look. "I'm fine. Just a little nervous, is all."

Hell, if he was just about to enter his family's house with a complete stranger pretending to be his significant other, he'd be a little nervous, too.

"Should we go inside?" he suggested.

"Yes, right. Inside." She glanced down at where his hand still rested on her arm. He started to withdraw it when she grabbed his fingers. "Oh, God, the rings."

She opened her purse and took out a small velvet pouch. Emptying the contents into her palm, she slipped a plain silver band on, then took his left hand in hers. She tried to ease the other, larger band onto his ring finger. The feel of her touching him, even for this innocuous purpose, ignited awareness wherever her fingers brushed his. She pushed the ring up to the second knuckle, but it refused to budge farther. He felt marginally relieved. Wearing a wedding ring for *any* reason didn't sit well with him.

"I don't understand. It fit Bill and you two are about the same height," she said half to herself.

"This is the real deal?" he asked, staring at the simple piece of jewelry. The guy had given up his wedding ring? He was coming to like Bill Burgess less and less.

Eva nodded and stared at his hand for a moment longer, then tugged the ring back off. "Never mind. I think I told my mother about the rings when we...when Bill and I got married, but if anyone asks, we'll just say you lost yours."

She swiftly moved her hands away from his. Adam

couldn't help wondering if she felt the same hot thrill he did whenever they touched.

"We could always say I gained weight and we haven't had a chance to get the ring enlarged yet."

Eva lifted her gaze to his and smiled softly. "Yes. I like that idea better."

She turned away from him and started for the door.

Adam joined her on the porch. He pushed up his glasses and tugged on the tight collar of his shirt. Was it him, or had the already sweltering temperature nudged up a couple degrees? How was it that he felt more nervous facing a family than he'd ever felt infiltrating armed-to-the-teeth militia groups? "You know, I'm still not exactly clear on how you want me to act—"

The door opened inward before Eva could touch the handle. Adam stared at a short, round woman who smiled warmly.

"Eva!"

Adam frowned. She'd said the name with a short *E* instead of the long *E* he and everyone else used. He turned the new pronunciation over in his mind, liking the sound of it.

"Mama." Eva hugged the woman tightly, then drew slightly away. "How's Papa?"

"Come in, come in, and see for yourself."

Eva hesitated. "Mama, I'd like to introduce my…husband."

Adam squared his shoulders and looked at Eva. He questioned the wisdom of something he'd had in mind ever since she told him to be himself. At any rate, there was nothing much she could do about it now, was there?

He stepped forward and thrust a hand forward. "Hello, Mrs. Mavros. I'm Adam."

4

"ADAM?" Eva's mother repeated, an I'm-sure-I-misheard-you expression creasing her face.

Eva wanted to die. Right then. Right there. Everything would be perfect if she could keel over now and never have to explain what she had done...what she was doing.

"Actually, it's William Adam," Adam said, digging a deeper hole, Eva was sure. A gigantic hole. A hole that would open up and swallow them whole any second. "Most people call me Bill, but I personally prefer Adam."

Eva stared at him, wondering if he'd broken more than his glasses back at that rest area in Virginia. She took in her mother's curious expression. Not much got past Katina Mavros.

That was it. The plan was foiled even before it got off the ground.

"Adam," her mother repeated, trying out the name and visually taking in the man on her front porch. "Yes, yes, Adam." Her dark eyes sparkled at Eva. "I prefer it, too."

Adam and Eve. Eva rolled her eyes. She didn't need to hear her mother say it aloud. The smile on her face said it all.

"Come in, come in." Katina Mavros warmly hugged him, then kissed him on both cheeks. "Welcome to the family, Adam."

She grasped his arm and practically dragged him inside the foyer, giving Eva a second to gather her scattered wits. Now she knew why she'd taken accounting in college rather than acting: she couldn't play a role to save her life. Obviously, neither could Adam even if he had fooled her mother.

This was all one huge, misguided mistake.

Dragging in a deep breath, Eva lay a hand against her stomach. She reminded herself that what she was doing wasn't entirely selfish. Besides, if she was right and her father was as ill as her mother had told her, this might be the last chance she had to try to make things right between them.

She closed the door behind herself, then moved toward the living room, where she was sure her mother had taken Adam. She froze at the sound of a familiar voice. A familiar, very *robust* voice that was saying something to her mother.

Eva entered the room to find Apostole Mavros looking much the same as the last time she'd seen him. Maybe even a little better, a weather-roughened cross between Marlon Brando and Anthony Quinn. His gaze met hers and his green eyes softened briefly. It was a moment Eva wished she could multiply and fill their entire strained relationship with. If not for her sake, for—

"Tolly," her mother reprimanded. "Is that any way to greet your son-in-law? Where are your manners?"

Recovering her own manners, Eva kissed her father's left cheek, then his right, then offered him her right cheek. She feared he was going to refuse returning the traditional greeting, then his dry lips brushed her cheek like a bayou breeze. She relaxed slightly.

"Hello, Papa." Eva moved back a couple steps. "How are you feeling?"

"Feeling?" he repeated, his ruggedly handsome face lined with a frown. "How should I be feeling?" He turned and slowly paced away, then returned, looking as surprised and confused as she felt. "My daughter comes home after not having visited for over a year, with no warning, telling me..." He gestured toward Adam who stood near the doorway. "Telling me this is the husband she married a year ago. A man we don't even know." He looked oddly sad, despite the small tinge of anger to his words. "How should I be feeling, Eva?"

With no warning? Eva sought her mother's gaze. Katina looked altogether too guilty.

Eva went still, a sick feeling settling into her stomach. She realized her own attempt at deception had placed her in the middle of another.

"You're not sick?" Eva turned back to her father.

"Sick?" her father said, repeating her words. "Why? Is this something you wish?"

"Of course he's not sick." Her mother rushed to Eva's side and whispered, "We'll talk about it later," before offering a louder, "What would make you think such a thing?" Katina Mavros stared at Eva meaningfully and took her arm. "You must be tired after your long trip. Why don't you and...Adam wash up before dinner?"

"Adam?" Her father repeated, eyeing the man standing in his living room.

Eva darted a glance in her "husband's" direction. She nearly groaned when Adam stepped awkwardly forward. She wanted to tell him no, not to offer his hand, but she was too late. Adam already had his arm out.

"Nice to meet you, Mr. Mavros. Eva has told me a lot about you."

Her father was silent, staring at the proffered hand Eva knew he would refuse to shake. Tolly Mavros was a man whose passions ran deep. Eva had seen him laugh more heartily than any person she'd ever known. She also knew he could be equally brusque when he was upset about something. And he was definitely upset.

Her father scratched his chin, looking Adam up and down. "What do you have in your hair that it looks so…sticky?"

"Sticky?" Adam repeated. "Oh, you must mean the gel. It's something I use to style my hair."

Tolly Mavros's stare was unwavering as he nodded his head.

Eva was glad her father didn't say anything more. Like make some fish-oil comparison or something else equally mortifying.

Funny, she'd never thought of Adam as genuine husband material, but now she couldn't help wanting to defend him as a wife should. That was good considering her short-term plan. Bad because her long-term one didn't include ever marrying again.

Adam dropped his hand and her father started from the room. He stopped halfway to the door, glanced at Eva, then at Adam, hmmphed and left.

Eva frowned. Patching things up with her father wouldn't be as easy as she had hoped. She supposed part of the reason was that their problems went back farther than her marriage. Much farther. Back to when she'd returned from college to find her accounting degree meant nothing to him. He had fully expected her to marry and bear him a dozen grandchildren. She shivered. After one month, she'd turned tail and run back to Jersey, where a few years later she had married someone she'd thought respected her for her mind, not for the birthing size of her hips.

Eva's mother waved her hand in the direction of the door. "Leave him be. He's not in a good mood today."

"He's never in a good mood."

Her mother raised her eyebrows and Eva tried to look a little repentant.

Unlike the strained relationship she shared with her father, she and her mother had kept close. In fact, it was likely as a result of that close relationship that Eva found herself in the middle of the bizarre situation she was in right now. She wanted to groan. She knew the instant she let it slip to her mother that she and Bill were having problems, she'd live to regret it.

Eva cringed to think what else her mother had planned.

"Mama, tell me right now what's going on," she said.

True to form, her mother ignored her first appeal. "Come now, and wash up. Everyone is waiting to see you and your husband."

"I'm not moving an inch until you do some explaining, Mama."

Her mother looked exasperated. She glanced at Adam before returning her attention to Eva. "Okay, okay, so I told a little white lie to get you down here. Is that so bad? You're here now, aren't you? And your father's not sick. Of that you should at least be glad."

"I am, Mama, but that's not the point."

"No, it isn't, is it?" Katina Mavros's sly smile made Eva even more uncomfortable with the game she was playing. "Now go on. I'm sure your husband would like to clean up after that long drive." Eva didn't budge. "Go on, go on. We'll talk later."

Katina smiled at Adam and he returned the gesture. Eva's gaze riveted on his mouth. Wide and generous and altogether too appealing. She'd caught a glimpse of that same smile when he'd turned it on Alice at work. But she'd been sure she was imagining things. Nerds weren't nerds only when they wanted to be.

Still, that thought didn't stop her from finding him somehow rakishly handsome when he smiled.

He turned to her and Eva felt something warm burst through her. Then the smile disappeared and he pushed up his glasses. The ones with the duct tape still holding the earpiece in place.

Suddenly, her mother's words finally registered. "Everyone? What do you mean everyone?"

Katina ushered her toward the steps. "You go upstairs. Adam can wash up downstairs."

"Mama," Eva warned.

"Well, go on. I swear, sometimes you can be as stubborn as your father."

Eva met Adam's gaze and he nodded toward the stairs, indicating she should go. She experienced a major attack of guilt for getting him into this mess. For Pete's sake, she was beginning to regret getting herself into it. But Adam appeared to be anything but a flailing fish out of water. She pushed her hair back from her face. In fact, if she didn't know better, she'd think her parents' actions had amused him.

She gave herself a mental shake. *That's ridiculous.* He's probably just in shock, that's all. At her mother's urging, she turned toward the stairs. *That's it. Adam Gardner is so surprised he doesn't know how to react.* But even as she hurried upstairs, she couldn't help thinking Adam had looked too calm. Too in control. He hadn't even blinked when her father had refused to shake his hand. He'd merely dropped his arm, his smile in place.

Few people could do that with style.

In the upstairs bathroom, Eva splashed her face with cold water. Just being in the large, five-bedroom, two-story home filled to the brim with Greek keepsakes and fishing memorabilia made her wish she lived nearby. She missed everyone terribly. An emotion all too easy to push aside in Jersey, but impossible to deny here. Despite everything, her roots were firmly planted in the damp, rich Louisiana soil. She'd even missed the sultry air that added a touch of thick expectation…suspense. As if there was no way something exciting couldn't happen in its own sweet time. That all she had to do was sit back and patiently wait for it. The way it felt in Jersey when a thunderstorm was brewing.

Curiously the comparison made her think of Adam. She vividly remembered how he'd looked in Virginia at the rest area, without his glasses, his hair mussed and sexy, his body hard and lean under her hands. The combination had caused a deep rumble within her—a rumble she could easily compare to distant thunder.

Abruptly, she pushed away the curiously provocative thought. Instead, she considered her options now that she knew her mother had tricked her into coming home.

She could leave. Since her father wasn't ill, she could grab Adam by the front of his geeky shirt, make some excuse about having a work emergency in Jersey and offer her farewells. She grimaced. What emergency could possibly exist in the life of an accountant? If one of her clients found themselves in any kind of trouble before or on Labor Day, they would call their lawyers, not her.

She was stuck. At least for tonight. Besides, she didn't think she could survive another twenty-hour drive without some major sleep first anyway. Tomorrow, however, offered all sorts of opportunities to come up with an excuse to get back on the road. Besides, she'd promised Adam that they would spend no more than a day here. Surely he would balk if they stayed longer.

She gave her dark hair a final check, then smoothed

her dress, making sure there wasn't a single thing out of place. She hadn't come to face her father's scrutiny. No. She was here to put Adam—her "husband"—in that particular spotlight.

She stepped into the hall and hesitated at the top of the stairs. The sound of gregarious voices and laughter drifted up to her. The "everyone" her mother mentioned earlier must mean the entire Mavros family. And dinner wasn't going to be a quiet affair, but a celebration of sorts to welcome back the prodigal daughter and her husband.

Husband.

Oh God, she'd left Adam to fend for himself. At this point, he was probably ready to rush for the door. Eva started down the steps, wishing she didn't feel as if she wanted to lead the way.

"*STEEN EYIA SAS.* That means to your and Eva's health." Eva's cousin offered the Greek toast, sweeping up his flat-bottomed wineglass. Adam briefly met Eva's gaze, then followed suit. She watched him toss back the inch-deep liquid with barely a grimace. She, on the other hand, had never gotten used to the piney essence of retsina. Her dislike of the wine was the perfect excuse to refuse more than an obligatory glass.

Her gaze drifted to where her father sat as always at the head of the heavy oak table in the dining room. He was slightly angled away from her, his food untouched, his meaty fingers tight around his wineglass though he had yet to drink any.

"Eat, eat," her grandmother said, nudging Eva's arm where she sat next to her.

Eva stared at her own barely touched food, knowing that she should try to eat. She took a nibble, then ignored the food on her plate, and the vast array of Greek and Creole food alike covering every inch of the table-top.

This was *not* going the way she'd planned.

Across the people-packed table Adam sat between her cousin and her uncle. And there had yet to be one prolonged, uncomfortable silence. Unless, of course, you were paying attention to *her* side of the table—that included her, her grandmother, her aunt and her unusually quiet brother, Pete—which no one was. Aside from some genuine interest in playing catch-up with her family, Eva found her gaze drawn time and again to the man across the table from her. The gel in Adam's hair had dried somewhat and a lock the color of a golden marsh reed fell across his forehead, covering the gray duct tape. While the glasses were bulky and ghastly, behind them she started to notice things she wasn't particularly sure she wanted to. Like the way his brown eyes sometimes held her gaze, a glimmer of unspoken challenge and wry humor giving him an aura of, well, sexuality.

Tilting her head, she rubbed her neck, suddenly hotter than she could blame on the high temperature and even higher humidity. Neither of which the whirling ceiling fan could ease. Her mother made another trip in from the kitchen, plunking down a large plate of steaming *tiropitas*—feta cheese pastries—directly in front of her.

"Eat, *ayapee mou.* I made them just the way you always like them," she said, stopping to squeeze Eva's shoulder, then passing to take her seat next to Tolly.

Distantly, Eva heard her father make that low-pitched hmmph. But she was too busy staring in horror at the mini-mountain of *tiropitas* to give his disapproval much notice. She was desperately trying to find a way to keep from seeing the Greek pastries she had always loved as a mound of raw dough that would sit like lead in her stomach. Her muscles clenched and her mouth gushed with saliva. Correction: the raw dough wouldn't sit like lead in her stomach...it would be the catalyst to chasing everything else out.

Oh, God.

"Excuse me." Eva pushed her chair back, nearly knocking it over as she rushed for the downstairs bathroom.

Long minutes later, she leaned against the sink, pressing a cool, damp washcloth against her burning face.

A soft knock sounded against the wood. Eva sighed. All she needed was her mother asking probing questions.

"I'll be out in a minute," she called with false cheer.

Fussing with her dress, she took a deep breath, then yanked the door open, a smile fixed on her face. Only it wasn't her mother she faced.

"Adam."

His small, concerned smile inexplicably irritated her. "Are you okay?"

"I'm fine."

Suddenly the hall seemed somehow darker than she remembered, and far more quiet. She heard herself swallowing. Her mother really should put in a hall light.

"I thought you were my mother." She tried to examine him more closely. "What are you doing here, anyway?"

"I thought going after you would be, you know, the husbandly thing to do."

"Not if you were anything like my ex." She took another deep breath. "Sorry, I didn't mean to say that. I..." She hesitated, directing her gaze everywhere but at his face. Which was difficult, seeing as the shaft of light from the bathroom dimly illuminated only him.

Why was he so tall? And why, suddenly, did she feel so…breathless near him?

"What happened back there?" he asked quietly, seeming far too close and smelling far too male. "Did you and something you ate do battle?"

Her gaze was drawn to his features. The indirect light deepened the shadows there, drawing out his cheekbones. Making the cleft in his chin seem even more attractive then ever. Something her grandmother used to say came rushing back. *Dimple in the chin, the devil within.*

She shifted her weight and dropped her gaze to his chest.

"I didn't eat anything," she said, stiffening.

"I noticed."

Eva frowned and eyed the man before her. The sound of the voices in the other room reminded her that neither of them were there to discuss her appetite, or lack thereof.

"Actually, Adam," she said, suddenly clear on what she needed to do. "Everything is not fine. You—" she jabbed her finger against his chest, surprised to find an enticing wall of muscle met her poke "—you are not fine. I'm not fine. In fact, no one here is fine."

She stared at the way his hair fell over his forehead.

"I…I don't understand," he said, pushing up his glasses.

"That's it! Why didn't you do more of *that* in there?" She pointed to his glasses. "Why didn't you act more like…like…"

She ran out of steam as she remembered a piece of their conversation in her office only yesterday.

"What, Eva?" His voice was way too low, almost seductive. "Like a geek?" His gaze dropped to her mouth. She turned her head, her pulse doing double duty. "Is that what you were about to say?"

Footsteps sounded in the adjacent hall and Eva's gaze fastened on Adam.

"Listen to me as I map this out for you, Adam. We're going to go back into that room, sit down, and in about five minutes I'm going to say I'm tired. That's when you're going to say you're tired, too. Then," she said, moving her head within inches of his. A bad idea when she felt his hot, wine-sweetened breath fan her cheeks. "Then we're going to go up to my room where we need to have a long talk."

"Talk? In your room?" His gaze dropped to her mouth.

"Uh-huh. Do you think you can remember that or do you want me to repeat it?"

Eva swallowed, wondering why Adam looked about ready to kiss her...and why she found the thought so very appealing.

AN HOUR LATER, exhausted and exasperated, Eva led the way upstairs, Adam following her. At least a dozen times she'd risen from the dinner table and announced she was tired. And a dozen more times, her plan had been thwarted—if not by Adam who had looked at her blankly, then by her family, who expected her to spend the whole night celebrating with them.

In fact, they would likely continue without her and Adam. All except for her father who had been notice-ably absent when they returned to the table earlier.

"I'm sorry," Adam said behind her for the fourth time since she'd practically hauled him from the din-ing room.

"It's okay," she answered again.

It must be the wine, Eva reasoned. The wine had short-circuited Adam Gardner's geek system. Turned him temporarily into a cohort in crime, conspiring against her every time she tried to get him to leave the table. Of course, it didn't take much to fall victim to the good-natured persuasiveness of her cousins. Eva allowed a fond smile. Still, for all the wine Adam had drunk, she'd think he'd at least be staggering. He wasn't.

Was Adam-the-nerd really Adam-the-lush?

She tossed a glance over her shoulder. No. Adam Gardner didn't strike her as the type to overly indulge in anything. Her gaze dropped to where he had undone the top two buttons of his shirt a little while ago. Her stomach muscles tightened as she remembered the way she had gaped at him. Recalled how he had captured her gaze and his lean fingers had frozen on the second button. As if her watching him unbutton his shirt was an intimacy he allowed few.

"We're in my old bedroom at the far end of the hall," she said softly. Given the direction her thoughts had been taking, the topic of bedrooms of any sort was a dangerous one. "It has its own bathroom that connects with the guest bedroom next door. But just in case, this is the other bathroom." She gestured toward the door to her right.

"Shouldn't we turn on the light or something? In case I need to find it in the middle of the, uh, night?" He reached in through the open doorway and flicked the light on.

Eva reached in and shut it back off. "I don't think you'll need it. I don't plan to sleep in the adjoining bathroom."

"Yeah, but maybe I should let you have that one. You know, in case you need it in a hurry." He turned the light on again.

Eva's cheeks burned, finding him much too close to her backside for comfort. Despite the moist Louisiana heat, or maybe because of it, she could feel Adam's own brand of warmth emanating off him in waves. It penetrated the thin material of her dress, making more than her stomach tighten.

"Don't worry," she said, trying to keep her voice even. "If you should happen to be in the bathroom when I need it, I can find this one. Unless, of course, you think *you'll* need it fast?" She shut the light off again.

"Me? Why would I...oh."

Eva slowly maneuvered to put herself at a safe distance, and with one well-directed glance, caught him up short.

"I've never gotten sick after drinking. I'm much too careful," he told her, but turned the light on again anyway.

"Yes, but I'd bet you've never had so much to drink before either."

"Actually..." His expression slowly shifted. "Yes, I guess you're right. I'm not much of a...partying person."

Partying person? Slowly, Eva switched the light back off. "Come on, before I forget what it is I wanted to talk to you about."

"Yes. Talk. I almost forgot."

Just like you forgot you were supposed to back me up when I wanted to leave the dining room, she thought. *And just like being around you, for some inexplicable reason, makes me forget that I don't need a man.*

At the end of the hall, Eva opened the door and threw on the light switch. She stopped dead in the doorway. Adam bumped into her from behind. The heat she'd felt coming from him before was nothing compared to the tangible touch of his body now.

A fiery jolt spread outward from the spots where he touched her; his rock-hard thighs against the backs of her legs, his wide chest against her back; the clear outline of his manhood grazing her bottom. She shivered, the searing sensation staying even when he moved slowly away.

Then her gaze riveted to the double bed in the middle of the room. An antique, wrought-iron canopy bed with double thick mattresses she feared she'd need a stepladder to reach.

One bed.

"We're in the wrong room," she whispered. Where were the two twin beds she'd always had? The extra bed she'd used when friends or cousins slept over? When Yaya gave up her room to visitors and slept in hers?

"Wrong room?" Adam skirted past her and went to stand in front of a bulletin board crammed with keepsakes. He fingered a faded pom-pom, an eyebrow rising above his glasses as he looked at her.

"Uh, Eva?"

Distantly, she noticed Adam was using the Greek pronunciation of her name. Her attention slowly shifted to him.

"I thought there was supposed to be twin beds," he said.

For the life of her, Eva couldn't help laughing. She forgot she didn't want him to pronounce her name that way. Gone was the tension she felt downstairs. Pushed even farther back was the memory of her mother practically hovering over her, catering to her every whim after she'd gotten sick. All she could concentrate on was the way Adam's forehead creased, and how he pulled at his open collar as if it were choking him.

"There used to be two twin beds," she said carefully.

"Then why does *that*," he said, pointing to the ornate bed that looked as if it belonged in one of the bordellos of New Orleans, "look like one bed?"

"Probably because it is, Adam." Eva peeked out the open door, then quietly closed it. For good measure, she switched on the ceiling fan, though she doubted it would do much for either the sweltering temperature in the room, or the restless heat building in her. Why couldn't her father budge from his old ways and get central air? She glanced back at Adam. Here *she* had been nervous when she first spotted the bed. Her reaction was nothing compared to the horrified expression on Adam's face.

She shrugged, wishing she could hold on to those light feelings, but the truth was, she was as concerned about sharing a bed as he was. Especially *that* bed. "I, uh, guess you're just going to have to sleep on the floor, Adam. I know that wasn't part of the bargain, but..."

Eva crossed the room to where someone had brought their luggage in. She evaded his gaze. Why was the tamest, safest man she knew turning out to be not so safe after all?

"I can't."

Frowning, she turned toward him. "You can't?"

"I can't."

"What can't you do, Adam?"

He pushed up his glasses. "Uh, sleep on the floor. I have...I have a bad back. While my chiropractor told me I need firm support, he nixed the idea of me sleeping on the floor."

The flicker of something in his dark eyes distracted Eva. Something that wasn't fear...wasn't quite regret.... She sighed, telling herself she was imagining things.

"Oh," she said absently. For reasons of her own, her sleeping on the floor was out of the question, as well. She looked from Adam to the bed, then back at Adam again.

"We could share the bed," he said quietly.

Eva stared at him. It was out of the question. Completely unacceptable. Insane, even. "Yes, I suppose we could try," she found herself saying instead. "We're both adults, right? And we're not in the least bit attracted to each other."

"Not in the least," Adam agreed with a wry smile.

"Right," she said, drawing the word out as if trying to convince herself.

She urged her attention back to her suitcase. Why had she thought one thing and said the other? And why did Adam look flatteringly pleased by her agreement?

She opened her suitcase to find it empty. "Yaya must have unpacked for us," she said, saying something, anything to break the charged, expectant silence in the room.

She opened the top dresser drawer. Her clothes were neatly folded inside. She sensed Adam's presence next to her before she saw him. He grasped her arms and roughly turned her toward him. She gasped. But instead of the passion she secretly hoped for, his expression was one of dark scrutiny.

"Somebody went through my stuff?"

5

DAMN, DID SHE FIND my gun?

Adam's gaze bolted to his open duffel bag on the floor next to her carryall, then down to where he still held Eva's upper arms. She blinked those green eyes of hers.

"Yaya didn't go *through* your things, Adam. She merely unpacked them, that's all."

He spotted his closed briefcase nearby and nearly groaned in relief. It would take a safecracker to get past the deceptively simple locks there. A vision of Eva's grandmother with a butter knife zipped through his mind, then vanished as he reminded himself he wasn't in the presence of hostile company. No matter how ill at ease he had felt when Eva's mother had hugged him when they first arrived. They were a normal, flesh-and-blood family. At least insofar as he believed such a thing existed. In fact, he found that the Mavros family were some of the nicest people he'd ever met, if you excluded Eva's crusty father. His own tension when he was around them, well, he'd just have to deal with it.

"Adam? Will you let go of me now?"

Eva's voice sounded strangely raspy and he looked down at her again. From this vantage point, he had a clear view of the deep V that formed the neck of her dress. Like him, she wasn't immune to the muggy climate. A dewy sheen covered her skin, a thin line of perspiration disappearing into the sweet valley between her breasts. Definitely not a view he got of her at work. He dragged his gaze up past her slightly open, tempting mouth to her eyes. The surprise, the touch of fear and the struggle for control he saw there were enough to make him bite back a curse.

Dumb move, Grayson. He berated himself for his brusque actions as he released her. First you accuse the woman's grandmother of something just this side of stealing. Now you're making no secret you'd like to push her onto the fantasy bed across the room and ravish her, starting with those luscious breasts. Not very geeklike behavior.

Eva leaned against the dresser for support, her flushed skin telling him she wasn't invulnerable to the sensations their touching had caused, either. Not very ice queen–like behavior. The image of her in that naughty bikini flooded back to him.

"Sorry," he said. A long distance separated Belle Rivage, Louisiana, and his boat docked in Delaware Bay off the coast of New Jersey. Not to mention the huge stretch between how he'd act as himself and as Adam the geek. "I just don't like anybody touching my things, that's all. Excuse me."

"What?"

He gestured toward the dresser to indicate he wanted access, and she slowly moved away. Which was a good thing, because if she hadn't, he would have touched her again. And this time, he wouldn't have stopped.

He opened the drawers, expending some of the sudden energy coiling in his muscles. Damn. How in the hell was he supposed to maintain his cover if this maddening woman could almost undo him with one unguarded glance?

He needed to get back into character. Now. Regardless of his personal fantasies, he had to stay focused on the fact that his presence here was strictly professional.

He was here to find out what Eva knew about her boss's illegal activities. And to determine what she knew about Oliver Pinney's disappearance. While he didn't make it a rule to separate business from pleasure, he got the distinct impression that pleasure with Eva might obliterate his business intentions. And for him, that would be a first.

In the dresser he ignored the red boxers stacked on top and took out his usual underwear before shoving the drawer shut again. He wanted to check his briefcase, but didn't dare add suspicion to the emotions plainly visible on Eva's flushed face.

She cleared her throat. "Do you suffer from one of those phobias where you're afraid of picking up diseases from everything you touch...or that touches you?"

"What?"

Eva gestured toward his clothes. "You said you don't like people touching your things."

She seemed genuinely concerned, but he noticed the way her back was a little too straight, her chin a little too jutted forward.

Get a grip, Grayson. Think geek.

"I like my things a certain way, that's all," he said a little too roughly.

Eva rested her right hand against the elegant curve of her neck, then turned toward the window that overlooked the front yard. "Oh."

"Do you want the bathroom first, or should I go?" He shoved his fake glasses up more out of frustration than the need to keep in character. The truth was, he wanted to take the damn things off and give Eva an undiluted view of the man he really was. The man who was on the verge of blowing his cover—and the whole damn assignment—just for a taste of her lips.

No, he couldn't show her *that* man. If he did, she

would likely throw him out. Then, not only his assignment would be shot to hell, but his ego would take a hell of a dent as well.

Still, he thought, eyeing how her pretty, yet innocuous dress clung to her figure, just because circumstances weren't the way he would have preferred, it didn't stop him from wanting to seduce her…even as Nerd Adam. The idea lingered in his mind, growing more appealing. He bit back a curse. Sure, up until now the challenges he allowed himself had been connected only to his job. Maybe he *was* missing out on a whole different ball game by resisting personal challenges. But seducing Eva was out of the question. No matter how much he wished differently.

"Mm, you go first," she said finally, turning from the window and dropping her hand to her side.

The suggestion that they could shower together drifted through Adam's mind, but since that idea fell under the heading "unsuitable," he moved toward the bathroom door.

"Adam?"

He glanced over his shoulder as he gripped the handle. "Yes?"

She gestured toward the door as he opened it. "That's the closet."

Adam stared at the plastic-covered garments hanging from a pole and bit back another curse. Not a shower in sight. He closed the door, wondering if impersonating a geek for too long could actually turn him into one.

THE LOCK on the connecting bathroom door slid home and Eva resisted the urge to lean against the white-enameled wood. She flushed anew. What did Adam think? She would walk in on him while he was taking a shower? Then again, this was the same guy who blew a gasket because her grandmother put his clothes away. She rested her hand against her burning cheek. She might even have smiled, if only the thought of walking in on him didn't appeal to her in a never-explored corner of her psyche. A corner she didn't want to explore.

She moved away from the door. What was it with her tonight? First she had reacted to his touching her in a way that completely baffled her, and now she was entertaining thoughts of voyeurism. It must be the hormones, she rationalized. Still, she couldn't help wondering what the broad-shouldered, rock-hard-thighed Adam would look like without clothes.

Closely monitoring the sound of the shower, she took her silk kimono-like robe out of the closet, then slipped out of her dress and put it on. Pulling the sash tight, she turned toward the bed. It's only for one night, she told herself. Besides, she was so exhausted, Mel Gibson could be lying beside her and she wouldn't know the difference.

Even as she tried to convince herself that she had nothing to fear from Adam, her attempts fell far short of the mark. Then she realized it wasn't Adam she was worried about at all—it was herself. Suddenly, she was overcome by odd feelings that gave spark to some interesting ideas she would never have considered twenty-four hours ago. The most shocking of which was the temptation to introduce the inexperienced Adam to the wonderful world of sensual sensation. To take off those glasses of his, muss the perfect part in his hair and guide his lean hands down her sweat-slick body. Show him exactly how a woman—how she—liked to be touched. Then there was the matter of touching him....

She climbed on top of the bed, and flopped across the firm mattress, fighting off the flash of yearning that accompanied her erotic thoughts. Of course, none of this made any sense whatsoever. She wasn't a seductress. She'd never given thought to doing anything near what was going through her mind. She'd worked with Adam for the past three weeks and had never thought of him as a...man.

She clamped her eyes shut. That wasn't entirely true. The quiet moment she'd first spotted Adam Gardner in the hall of Sheffert, Logan and Brace, when no one else was around, something unaccountable had stirred in her. Then *he'd* seen *her*, pushed up his glasses, his posture had slumped, and he'd smiled in a sheepish way that had wiped all interest from her mind.

Until now.

The shower switched off in the other room. Eva slid off the bed and smoothed the white coverlet. Rushing across the room, she hauled her briefcase to the desktop where she'd spent many a teenage night studying. Behind her, the door opened.

"I hope I didn't take too long."

Eva waved her hand. "No, no, you're fine. I was just going over some work things anyway."

"It's all yours," he said.

Not daring to look at him, she turned away, collected her nightgown, then practically dived into the bathroom without so much as a glance at him. She pulled the door closed so quickly that a puff of humid air blew her hair from her face. But that slight breeze did little to cool her overheated body.

ADAM UNDERSTOOD Eva's refusal to get involved again—with anyone. It was a natural defense mechanism considering she was recently divorced. And her lunge for the bathroom without a glance in his direction verified his assessment.

In hindsight, he wished he had done the same, and

kept his gaze away from her. Instead, he presently stood in the middle of her childhood bedroom, an erection painfully pressing against the fabric of his briefs, and wondered at the exact cause of his reaction to her. Both earlier and now.

Oh yeah, he had admired, even mildly fantasized about, Eva Burgess's legs. But that had been at work, with her wearing panty hose, shoes and knee-length skirts. Seeing those same legs bare, silky smooth, tanned and seeming to go on forever, he had been sorely tempted to cross that line between business and pleasure, attraction and undercover flirtation, to find out exactly how high up those legs went. Satisfy a sudden hunger to explore the soft, warm flesh that lay where her legs ended.

His response to Eva was unexpected not because she managed to get him so worked up, and certainly not because of his job-imposed abstinence. It was because his reaction wasn't the kind that just any woman could satisfy. No. He strongly suspected his response was uniquely tailored to Eva Burgess. And it would be only Eva Burgess who could satisfy it.

He stepped to the window and stared out at the dark night, trying to make out the road. He tried harder still to sort out the tension that filled him. Ever since that guy broke into Eva's car, he'd been on edge. And the feeling had only increased throughout the evening.

Crossing purposefully to the closet, he yanked open the door.

"I'd better find something to put on," he muttered to himself, cursing the short time between Eva's bizarre request at work, and her picking him up at his apartment, leaving him no opportunity to buy pajamas. Hell, normally he didn't even wear briefs to bed. But Eva didn't know that. And she wouldn't unless he wanted to spend the night on the floor.

Jerking through the plastic-protected clothes hanging in the closet, he told himself Eva would expect him to wear something—anything—to bed. But in truth, he didn't want to be vulnerable to the unfamiliar emotions significantly attached to his attraction to the woman in the other room.

He drew in a deep breath then released it with a low hiss. Nothing. Not one single thing that was long enough to stretch over his six-foot height, much less wide enough for him to get into. He touched what looked like a quilted winter robe he guessed—he hoped—belonged to Eva's grandmother, then closed the closet door.

His gaze settled on the desk in the corner and the laptop that sat on it.

His mind slowly shifted gears. Glancing at the closed bathroom door, he stepped toward the desk and flicked up the laptop's LCD screen. A brief search for the Honeycutt diskettes came up short. Holding down the button to switch on the computer, he clicked his way out of the menu driver and started a global search of the hard drive.

He glanced at the bathroom door again. Still closed, shower still running.

There were many of what appeared to be business-related files, but Eva's file names were ambiguous, a bunch of letters and consecutive numbers. When he tried to view them, the computer's operating system told him they were password-protected.

"Adam, what are you doing?" Eva said quietly.

He didn't move. Didn't bat an eye. Experience had taught him never to start at a surprise. To offer no outward sign that he'd been caught doing anything suspicious. Especially when he could easily explain away his actions. That training worked perfectly as Adam covertly touched the keys that would put him back into the main menu driver, then looked in Eva's direction.

She stood in the bathroom doorway, her dark hair even darker wet, the sound of the shower coming from the open doorway.

Damn. He offered a sheepish smile and pushed up his glasses. "This is some laptop. I hope you don't mind, but I couldn't resist seeing what power that baby...er, it has."

For long moments she stood there, looking at him, glancing at the computer, looking as if she didn't know whether to believe him.

"I've been shopping for one for myself. I mean, I have a PC at home, of course...."

"Of course."

He was going to have to come up with more than that. "Well, since I got this job, I can finally afford a new one. But there are so many of them. I can't seem to decide which one to get."

Adam noticed she'd changed from the skimpy, all-too-sexy robe and now wore what he could only describe as the nightgown from hell. An opaque white-and-rose print material, tentlike and stitched up the whazoo with pink piping and virginal lace that covered every piece of her tantalizing flesh.

"Damn" was what he wanted to say.

"I...I hope you don't mind my taking a look." He motioned toward the laptop that was still on. He frowned and pushed up his glasses again. "I mean, I'm sorry if you thought I was invading your privacy or anything, because I wasn't."

What would she say if she knew at that moment, even with her wearing that...that *thing* she had on, he wanted to invade far more than her privacy?

She crossed the room and closed the screen of the laptop. "I'd have appreciated it if you'd asked first."

The tantalizing smell of perfumed soap and clean fe-male flesh teased his nose.

"Would it be too forward to ask if I might use it this weekend? For work purposes, of course." He offered a grin he hoped would push her right past the wariness painted all over her face. "And to see if it can handle me, you know, if I decide I want to buy a similar one."

A reluctant smile turned up the side of her magnificent little mouth. "Sure, go ahead. You can probably communicate with it better than I can anyway. Maybe you can explain a few things to me about what it can do."

Good. He'd have free access to her laptop. That would certainly make his investigation easier. If there was anything in that computer about Sheffert's dirty dealings, he'd find it. He only wished that finding such proof wouldn't mean she was in on it.

"Uh, Eva, didn't you forget something?" he asked, pointing toward the bathroom. Why had she left the shower on, anyway?

"Oh." She passed him again and he nearly groaned at her enticing scent as she hung the dress she'd been wearing earlier on a hanger, put it in the bathroom, then closed the door. "I want to steam the wrinkles out," she explained.

Leave it in here and in a few minutes I'll generate enough heat to iron the wrinkles out of a sharpei.

Finally her expression shifted as she eyed him. And Adam suddenly realized he'd completely forgotten about putting something on.

FROZEN, yet, strangely, feeling as if she was suffering from heat exposure, Eva's gaze began at Adam's feet, then worked its way up. Past lean, golden hair–covered calves. Over delectable thighs. Dragging in a breath, she skipped up farther to a hard, well-toned stomach she could do laundry on. Over pecs as defined as any weight lifter's. Past arms that could protect a woman from storms and muggers alike.

Then, unable to resist, her gaze slid back down. Her breath choked off altogether. He wore the athletic type of Jockeys that stretched down to his hard thighs, the top band firmly around his waist. But that they covered more than others didn't much matter; what did was the snug way they fit around his…manhood. And the thin cotton did little to conceal the long, solid ridge of an erection.

Eva turned away, her cheeks burning. A surprising, hot need erupted deep in her stomach.

She swallowed…hard.

"I, uh, forgot to bring my pajamas."

Eva jerked her gaze up to Adam's face, where she vowed to keep it. "Pajamas. Right."

Putting pajamas on this man would be a definite crime to society, she thought as her scrutiny dipped back to his gorgeous torso.

"I usually wear my royal-blue ones on the weekend," he said. "They're cotton so they don't itch, and have these stripes down the front.…"

Eva didn't understand what he was saying. Royal blue? Stripes? Oh, pajamas. She forced her errant gaze back up to his face and found him pushing up his taped-together glasses. Then her gaze dipped down a second time. Her thoughts threatened to veer out of control all over again.

She cleared her throat. "Work out, do you, Adam?"

"Excuse me?"

Giving him a long, obvious look, Eva smiled. "I asked if you work out."

"Oh, yes. Yes, I do, a little. Does it show?" He glanced down at himself.

Oh, God. Yes, it definitely showed.

"Here, let me see if I can't find something for you to wear." Like a suit of armor, she thought as she opened the closet door. After a long search, she came up with nothing. It appeared the only thing that would fit him was what he had on…or his polyester slacks and one of his button-down shirts. And he certainly wouldn't be comfortable wearing his clothes all night. Even if his wearing clothes to bed would certainly make *her* feel more comfortable.

"Well," she said, resigning herself to the fact that she was just going to have to control her raging hormones. "I can't find anything, so your, um, underwear is going to have to do." She looked away. "Anyway, I think it covers enough of you to be considered decent."

Decent? Now, that was laughable.

"If you're sure."

She wasn't sure. "I'm sure."

For long minutes, Eva busied herself. She turned off the shower. Folded down the coverlet on the bed. Then crossed to go to her desk, past where he still stood in the middle of her very feminine room looking very masculine despite his geeky glasses.

She could handle this. She *had* to handle this.

"Before we call it a night, Adam, I think it's a good idea to have that talk I mentioned." She scanned the room. Not even her old desk chair was here to sit on.

Instead, she crossed to the bed and started to pat the spot next to her. She changed her mind and motioned to the other side of the mattress. No sense testing herself unnecessarily.

The mattress moved under his weight and Eva fought the urge to see how his underwear fit now.

She cleared her throat. "I guess I didn't make myself clear on the trip down," she said awkwardly, running her finger along the hand-stitched design on the coverlet. "My entire reason for bringing you here was to make my family *not* like you."

There was a heartbeat of a pause. Then he said, "I don't get it. Not like me?"

She glanced at him, wondering if he intended to sleep in those glasses. "Yes."

He frowned. "We're back to that geek thing again, aren't we?"

Yes. "No, no, this has nothing to do with my thinking you're a…geek, Adam. Because I don't. Think you're a geek, I mean." She realized she was babbling, but she couldn't help herself. He shifted, bringing his body closer than she was comfortable with. She swore she could feel the heat of his skin just inches away from hers. Her pulse leaped. "I thought by not telling you much about the situation here, or what I expected of you that…" She drifted off for a moment, then, "Basically, most people wouldn't have reacted as well as you did to my family…my father in particular."

"I see."

Eva could see that he didn't.

"I was afraid of this," he said, staring at his fingernails. Nails that were manicured and neat, attached to fingers that were long and lean, in line with the rest of his body. "I should have insisted you be more specific in what you expected of me."

"You did. Insist, I mean," she said, tugging her hands away from the coverlet when she nearly touched his knee. "I was the one who should have listened."

He shifted, obviously uncomfortable again, putting him nearly in the middle of the suddenly too-narrow double bed. Eva almost jumped.

"Look, Adam," she said, trying to gather her scattered wits, "my mother said my father is going to work tomorrow. It's the perfect opportunity for us to leave."

Ultimately, Eva had to face facts. And the facts were that this plan was a complete and utter failure. She would have to find another way to try to bridge the gap between her and her father.

"You want to leave without saying goodbye to him?"

Eva closed her eyes, realizing how crass that sounded. "No. No, I guess I don't. But there's no reason we can't leave after he comes back. I mean, he's not sick as I was led to believe, thank God...." She moved closer to the edge of the mattress, his nearness seeming to give off some sort of electrical signal that threatened to short-circuit her thought processes. "I guess what I'm trying to say, Adam, is that I want you to be clear on how to act when you do say goodbye to him."

She met his gaze and found the desire to slip those hideous glasses down his straight nose almost irresistible. She resisted. Because it was the right thing to do. Because the feelings swirling through her body were all too new, too unfamiliar, and had developed too rapidly for her to trust.

"I never meant to imply that you were a geek, but I'm hoping that maybe you could..." He shifted even closer. "That you could act like one. You know, for his benefit."

"I see."

This time she saw that he did. In fact, she saw far more than that. She saw that he looked about ready to kiss her.

"Tell me, Eva," he said in a voice that wasn't Adam-like at all. A voice that slid over her hot, hypersensitive skin like a hand, urging to life emotions she had vowed to keep at bay. "If we should ever be placed in a position where we should have to kiss—"

"We won't," she whispered, her throat unbearably

tight. "It's not Christmas, and there's no, um, mistletoe or anything."

She shivered as his gaze homed in on her mouth.

His own lips turned up at the corners. "Just the same, assume for the sake of argument there is a time when kissing is…expected from us…" His mouth moved ever closer, nearer to hers, riveting Eva's gaze to the well-defined line of his lips. "How, exactly, should we do it?"

Eva knew she should move away from him, turn her head, do something, anything to prevent what was about to happen. But the simple truth of it was that she wanted this kiss. She wanted it to happen as much as Adam seemed awkwardly determined to make it happen. And she wanted it *now*.

Wresting the initiative from him, she stopped the slowly seductive way his head tilted toward hers by pressing her lips tentatively against his. Then she gave in fully to the part of her that made her kiss him in the first place.

He tasted of toothpaste, a bit of wine, and hot, hot desire. With the tip of her tongue, she brazenly sought a more intimate taste, aroused by the way he opened his mouth slightly and invited her tongue in.

Need rushed over Eva in swells, carrying pleasure signals to her limbs. She reached out and braced her hands against his solid shoulders, but the touch evolved into a caress, the caress a bold exploration of the marvelous muscles that made this man oh so much more than an inexperienced nerd.

He had yet to touch her, and Eva found she yearned for that more than anything. Wanted to feel his hand against her heated flesh, needed him to touch her in a way she suspected he hadn't touched another woman.

She rested her hand against his clean-shaven cheek, placing the tip of her thumb in the dimple in his chin.

Then she deepened the kiss, plunging her tongue deep into his mouth, urging his into hers. Her breathing became a rapid, urgent search for the air she couldn't seem to get enough of.

She stroked her fingers down his incredibly muscled arms and reached for his hands. Tugging on his hand, she met opposition.

"Eva, I, um, don't think—"

"Shh." She compensated for his slight resistance and led his fingers to the top of her nightgown. She pressed her breast into his palm. The heat of his skin penetrated the thin cotton and shock waves of pleasure shot through her, pushing aside any doubt about what she was doing, infusing her with an ever-growing need for more.

His palm stayed, unmoving, on her breast. She strained against it, her nipple hard and aching, the increasingly demanding cadence of her kiss telling him she wanted more, much more.

Dragging her lips to his jaw, she flicked the tip of her tongue in and around the delicious dimple in his chin. Then down to trace the clean line of his collarbone. She moved lower still to catch a nipple between her teeth, teasing it with her tongue. Her fingers sought the waistband of his briefs. She tugged at them impatiently, slipping her fingers in until they touched the silky, hot, hard length of him. She curled her fingers around his arousal and ran her thumb over the sensitive tip. Finding a bead of moisture there, she rubbed it down the length of him. Adam bucked against her. His reaction prodded her on. She began a slow, concentrated stroke designed to push him beyond his limits in a way she guessed no one ever had.

"Eva—"

"Adam…just be quiet and touch me."

Eva removed her hand from his Jockeys and plied

his mouth with her tongue, coaxing him to return the kiss, pleading with him to finish what she had started. All she knew was the incredible need within her to be satisfied…to obtain the release he promised her with his kiss, his nearness.

Something seemed to give within Adam and the fingers at her breast slid to her waist. Eva groaned in protest, thinking she had scared him away with words that shocked even her, until he glided his hand back up to cup her breast and rubbed a teasing thumb over her nipple. She shuddered.

Acting on every instinct that at any other time would set off warning alarms for her to run the other way, Eva urgently bunched her nightgown up to the tops of her thighs and straddled him. She hated when the movement interrupted their kiss, but was gratified when their mouths met again.

Adam pushed her away slightly and did away with his glasses. Eva was too filled with need to concentrate on anything more than the ball of heat spiraling within her. Adam's fingers dug into the flesh of her thighs and hauled her forward until she rested against his erection. The action forced a gasp from Eva's throat. The knowledge that there was nothing more than his Jockeys and her panties separating them further fed the fire within her…until a rush of awareness made her take another look at the fact that *nothing more than his Jockeys and her panties separated them.*

Adam's fingers moved from her breasts and inched lower and lower still, until he'd slid his fingers into the top of her panties, finding the tangle of hair beyond.

Eva dragged her mouth from his and quickly trapped his fingers with her hand. She rested her forehead against his cheek, suddenly staggered by what she was doing, what she had done.

"Oh, God. This is…this is insane." Eva gasped for

breath, grasped harder still for a handle on a situation that had reeled so completely out of control.

Not daring to meet his gaze, she twisted away from where she straddled his hips. She tried not to look at the way his erection still pressed against the thin material of his briefs, but was unable to help herself.

"I…" She pushed her hair from her burning face. She what?

Eva lifted her gaze to find he'd put his glasses back on. His hair was tousled and sexy from where she'd run her fingers through it, and very blond without the gel he usually applied. The contrast between the nerd she had thought she was safe with, and the man who had awakened a frightening, insatiable need within her, was dizzying. She clutched at the buttoned neck of her nightgown, making sure it was tightly closed.

"I gotta tell you, Eva, if that's what's going to happen if we ever have to kiss in front of your family, I think we should avoid it at all costs." Adam's voice was low and husky, and he looked very un-geeklike with his intense, passion-filled expression.

Eva flushed anew, her body still yearning for the man a foot away from her.

She looked down and found her nightgown had roamed up and was bunched around her waist. She pulled it down to cover her overheated, bare skin.

He ran his hands over his head several times, smoothing his hair back, making him look more like the man she could deal with. Or at least the man she had thought she could deal with. At any rate, his looking more like the nerd she had enlisted would make it easier to deal with him in the way she had to. Which was to keep him and the situation as impersonal as possible. And that didn't include wrapping her fingers around his straining…

"Tell me something, Eva. Why did you start that if you had no intention of finishing it?"

"What do you mean?" she asked. "You were the one who started talking about kisses...."

"Yes. And you were the one who kissed me." He cleared his throat and some of the roughness left his voice, but not much. "Not that I mind, you see. But a man isn't a faucet you can just turn on and off at will."

Faucet? Man? Eva's gaze slipped over his toned physique then she forced herself to focus on his face and his big, bulky glasses. No, Adam didn't look a bit like a faucet. He did, however, seem very much a man.

Lifting a hand to her neck, she said, "I'm sorry. That should never have happened."

He was silent for a long moment. "Why?"

She swallowed hard. "Because I'm pregnant."

EVERYTHING ABOUT this was *wrong*. Wrong, wrong, *wrong*. Despite what Adam's body was telling him.

Lord, he had only meant to tease her as Adam the geek, a desire that had proved unwise. But there had been no way to foresee what had just happened between them.

And what had happened?

You lost control, that's what. And you never lose control. You can't afford to lose control. You're on assignment.

Still not trusting himself, but needing to see that she had actually said what he thought she'd said, he shifted his gaze to Eva's expressive face. Her words finally registered.

She was pregnant.

"What?" he asked.

"I said, I'm pregnant."

He sat back, scanning her from head to foot. No way, no how did she look pregnant. Weren't pregnant women supposed to be bloated, their bellies swollen, their skin splotchy…and weren't they supposed to be married? He rubbed the back of his neck, grimacing at the stupid last thought. Well, at the very least, she should have to wear some sort of letter, the equivalent of Hester Prynne's own *A*, to let everyone know her condition. At least until it showed on its own. Let the man know *before* they were just seconds away from lovemaking that she was about to become a mother.

Adam groaned. That thought was even more bizarre than the other. He glanced at Eva. While she was still obviously shaken by what had happened between them, she was also looking at him closely. Too closely.

Deflect and redirect. Isn't that what he'd been taught during his first weeks as a field agent? In an uncomfortable situation, deflect any suspicion and redirect it toward your opponent. And sure, while he probably should draw on the inexperience expected by the Adam persona he had created, his mind had ceased functioning somewhere between her pressing his palm against her breast, and her hand slipping inside the waistband of his skivvies. Damn but he had dangerously miscalculated the depth of passion of which this woman was capable. More than that, he had severely underestimated the ferocity of his own response to her.

But she's pregnant, he reminded himself.

God, but this whole situation was weird. And while his instincts told him he should stay in character, awkwardly laugh the whole thing off in some nerdlike way, the real Adam wanted some answers, and he wasn't going to stop until he got them.

"Wait a minute. Didn't you say you were divorced?"

"What?" Eva's well-kissed mouth finally worked around the one-word reply. "Of course I'm divorced."

She looked for all the world as baffled as he felt.

"Look, the last thing I wanted to happen, expected to happen, was this," she said. And he believed her. She carefully stretched the material of her nightgown to cover her toes. "I meant it when I said I'm not interested in getting involved with anyone. Now you know why."

Pregnant. In hindsight, Adam supposed he should have had her condition pretty much pegged when she pulled over on the drive down and killed the weeds at the side of the road. Then a couple other facts came together. Like her avoidance of caffeine. Her odd request that he impersonate her husband.

Still, given the facts she'd laid out for him the day before, the last thing he'd have expected was that Eva Burgess was pregnant.

He eyed her, trying to make some sort of sense out of the situation. "Your parents don't know yet, do they? Not just about the divorce, but about your pregnancy?"

Why not tell her parents she had divorced a man they had never met? *Because that man is the father of the child she carries.*

While the fact that she was pregnant at all should have barred any thought of physical intimacy from Adam's mind, oddly he still found himself drawn to her. Having had a taste of her sweet, hot mouth, having touched her, he wanted more.

"No, I haven't told my family about the baby. Not yet," Eva said quietly.

He searched her face. "Why?"

"Because..." She clamped her eyes shut and Adam used the opportunity to take in everything that was her. The thick dark hair that curled around her face and shoulders like a dark storm cloud. That...that mouth that had the power to undo him with a single, electrifying kiss. Those hands that she gestured passionately with and those same hands' ability to seek out his most fundamental passions. Drawing them to the surface, bringing him to within moments of nirvana.

"God, everything seemed to make so much sense yesterday," she said, opening her eyes. Sexy, olive green eyes that said a lot but left out more. "I wanted to set the groundwork for inevitable divorce before I dropped the bomb that I was pregnant with a child whose father would never be a part of my baby's life."

Adam narrowed his eyes, his gut tightening. "Your choice or his?"

Her expression was wary, yet was still shadowed with the passion they had shared mere moments before. She pushed off the bed, making sure that hideous nightgown of hers covered every inch of her delectable skin.

"I don't want to discuss it." She turned away from him. "Look, I never intended to tell you as much as I have. Trust me, you don't want to know my story of woe."

But he did. Adam got off the bed, too, not ready to explore the reasons for that one. In his job, it was dangerous to grow personally attached to anyone involved in a case. While he always asked the questions necessary to keep his undercover roles safe, none included "Tell me, why doesn't your ex-husband want to be a father?" And the rancor he felt that an innocent would suffer from the selfishness of its own parents had nothing to do with his assignment.

He paced across the room, trying to regain control over a situation that was a first for him.

He glanced over to find Eva going through her attaché case. The fact was that while Eva's name was the equivalent to the Biblical Adam's Eve, she was in no way, shape or form *his* Eve. For one, she had already taken a hefty bite out of the forbidden apple. Two, he had figured out long ago that, for him, there was no

Eve, or Eva, or a life mate by any other name, becaus
there was no such thing as happily-ever-after. Not i
his life. Not in the lives of anyone he knew. His com
mitment was to his job. And it was going to stay tha
way.

No matter what happened, he wouldn't allow Ev
and her passionate ways to tempt him away from tha
decision.

"Look, this whole plan is one, huge mistake," Ev
said. Giving up her attempt at normalcy, she face
him. "I'm going to go to the guest room next door an
make up the bed for you. If anybody finds out, so be i
I'll just tell them the truth."

Adam warily eyed her. "The truth is good."

"If only I knew what the truth was anymore."

Eva murmured the thought just as a similar on
wandered through Adam's mind. He surveyed her
but she was already moving toward the bathroom, pre
sumably to gain access to the room next door. The mo
ment she was out of view, he slowly shook his head
He must have imagined her words.

EVA TRIED the door handle a second time. Locked. Sh
pressed her forehead against the cool wood, strugglin
with the desire to curse her mother and grandmother
After all their manipulations, she held out little hop
that the hall door to the guest room would be un
locked. If only she hadn't told her mother about th
problems she and Bill were having… As it stood, sh
didn't doubt her mother and grandmother were tryin
to reconcile her marriage. If only they knew it was al
ready beyond reconciliation. And that the man in th
other room was not only *not* her husband or the fathe
of the baby she carried, but he was almost a complet
stranger.

She stood there shivering though it was unbearabl

hot. She touched her fingers to her swollen lips. The tiny action sent warm emotion curling through her. If asked to explain what had happened in the other room, she would be hard-pressed to offer anything that would make any sense, except that she'd wanted Adam Gardner's kiss more than she'd wanted anything in a long, long time.

The new sensations clung to her like the humid air. They clamored for a satisfaction she could only fantasize about. A fulfillment of a need she had sworn she'd deny.

Certainly Bill Burgess hadn't touched what Adam had awakened in a few sweet minutes. She thought he had, once. But not anymore. And that, more than anything, should have scared her.

Her hand slid down over her stomach, resting over the slightly rounded area that would soon swell with the growth of the baby within. A baby whose father had sworn he'd have nothing to do with his offspring when Eva had told him she was pregnant.

Oddly enough, not even her maternal feelings for her baby, or her vow to protect him or her from the pain of rejection, were enough to quell the almost savage desire still running through her. It was as if some deep, fundamental part of her she had yet to identify was acting on a primal need to find a mate who would protect her. Love her. Provide her with everything she would ever need for the rest of her life. And care for her child as she would. A hunger based not on financial requirements, but on the basic, human need to be loved. The need to explore all the fascinating facets of being a woman, of being alive, of learning exactly what life itself was all about.

And as incongruous as it seemed, the socially inexperienced man in the other room had been the one to set off those feelings. Feelings she had to tamp down and bury if she held out any hope of staying true to her vow never to allow another man to hurt her or her baby again. Loving any man posed that risk. *Including* the man in the other room.

Eva closed her eyes and released a ragged breath. The guest-room door was locked. Where did she go from there?

Simple, her ever-practical side told her. *You just give Adam a pillow and tell him to camp out on one of the sofas downstairs until you can figure all this out.*

Oh yes, that would be very generous of her. Drag the guy all the way to Louisiana, then tell him he and his bad back had to fit themselves onto a sofa long enough to hold half his height. All because she had wanted a kiss that had turned into so much more.

She swallowed hard. *She* could always sleep on the sofa.

A vision of her father shaking her awake and asking questions she would be hard-fought to answer when she was lucid loomed in her mind.

Besides, judging by the occasional scrape of a chair leg against the floor downstairs, the family celebration had indeed gone on without her and Adam. And it likely wouldn't end until well into the early-morning hours. What would she do until then?

"Eva?"

She started and swung around to face Adam where he stood just inside the bathroom.

"Your mother's at the bedroom door."

"Good." Careful not to make any type of physical contact with Adam, Eva strode from the too-small bathroom. This was the perfect opportunity to explain to her mother what was and was not going on and demand the key to the room next door.

"Mama, you and I have to talk." She hauled the door open.

Her mother furtively glanced into the room, apparently trying to see if things between her daughter and son-in-law were going well. A tug of regret pulled at Eva's heart.

"Eva, honey? Are you going to be long?" Adam said from behind her.

Eva slowly turned to find Adam lying in the decadent wrought-iron bed, the crisp white top sheet draped over his hips in a way that hinted he wore nothing, but was covered enough to be decent.

Decent. There was that word again.

Her mother took in the scene. When her gaze slipped back to Eva's face, her eyes sparkled with mischief. "Good, you two have settled in. I just wanted to stop in to say good-night."

Eva's cheeks burned as her mother kissed them. Somehow, she managed to return the warm gesture, the tug on her heart growing more pronounced.

It's going to break her heart when she learns I'm divorced.

Eva said good-night and her mother quietly closed the door.

6

EVA WOKE SLOWLY, aware of Adam's absence even before a glance verified it. The hazy morning sun warming her face told her the day was going to be hotter than the previous one. She pushed her damp hair from her cheeks and glanced at the twisted, empty sheets next to her. While the day itself might get hotter, she resolved that matters between her and Adam needed some definite cooling off.

She propped herself up on her elbows. The only sound was the gentle humming of the ceiling fan. She wasn't sure what time she finally drifted off to sleep. The world had been shadowy and still, and the last car had long since driven away. And she hadn't dozed off until long after she'd come to terms with the fact that she'd made her bed with her impulsive little plan, and now would have to literally lie in it.

She simply wished that lying next to Adam in this bed, feeling his heat, listening to his even breathing, wasn't part of the bargain.

She picked up the pillow he had used and crowded it against her breasts, inhaling the smell of him. The subtle odor of soap, and the tangy essence that was his, and his alone.

Groaning, she plunked the pillow down then peeled the sheet away from her traitorous body. The sheet was the sole thing that had come between her and Adam the night before. And that was merely because he had thought it a good idea that he slept on top of it, while she slept underneath. At the closet, Eva reached for a sundress, thinking the sheet hadn't been the only thing that had kept them apart. Aside from her own need to get a grasp on what had passed between them last night, Adam appeared to grapple with a struggle of his own.

She had little doubt that her pregnancy was the cause. That detail should have kept *her* away from him. But it hadn't. The resulting emotions left her feeling hurt, upset, and longing to understand both herself and his reaction to her news.

She took the dress with her into the bathroom, then turned on the shower and slipped out of the damp nightgown. She needed to distance herself from these unfamiliar sensations that lingered. Escape the heat clinging to her, inside and out. She lathered the soap and switched her analyzing skills on Adam. She stumbled across more than a few interesting questions.

Why had he kissed her? No matter the excuse he had offered, Eva believed he had kissed her for pleasure's sake alone. And despite his mild protests at her venturing to take things further, he had been inching toward just that when she stopped him. If she hadn't emerged from the longing-induced stupor she'd been in, would he have made love to her? Would he have done so if he'd known she was pregnant with another man's child?

Eva stepped under the shower spray, welcoming the momentary thought-robbing cold spray of water.

No, she determined. No man could have gone ahead after hearing that bit of news. No man could desire her enough not only to accept her condition, but to embrace it. Not even Adam.

Besides, she couldn't see Adam making love to her after only twenty-four hours of getting to really know each other. She lethargically washed, rinsed then turned off the shower. But what, exactly, *did* she know about Adam?

She searched for something, anything he had offered about his own family. His past, his friends, a pet, *anything*. And came up with little more than he had a neighbor who threw clothes out of apartment windows, and that he had a crush on her laptop.

Thinking about it, the whole situation seemed more than strange…it was *abnormal*. Sure, maybe Adam felt awkward discussing personal matters, but so did she. Especially given how very personal hers were. Yet he now knew about her pregnancy, and had managed to coax information from her about her ex-husband and her family.

There was a knock at the outer door. Slipping into her dress, Eva entered the bedroom to find her mother walking in.

"Good, you're up," she said. "I was afraid I was going to have to send your grandmother in to wake you for breakfast."

Eva's stomach lurched. "Where's Adam, Mama?"

Her mother glanced at her. "Adam? You mean you don't know?"

"Know what?"

Her mother pulled back the sheet to make the bed and Eva urged her away.

"Know what, Mama?" she said more firmly. Given what her mother and grandmother had done so far, Eva tensed, preparing for the worst.

"Your father took Adam oystering with him this morning."

What? "What?"

Katina Mavros could have said anything else. That Adam had left. That he had spilled the truth to her family about their fake marriage and everybody was waiting for her corroboration. But this bothered her more than all the other possible answers combined. Except for his employees, her father never took anyone oystering with him.

"Yes, isn't that nice?"

"Nice?" No, it was awful. Eva felt a twinge of something she could only liken to jealousy. Which was childish at best. But somehow that's the way she always felt around her father.

Tolly Mavros had never taken her oystering.

She curled her fingers around a bedpost and rested her forehead against the cool iron.

Her mother quietly watched her. "Come now, let's have breakfast. I cooked up a little something for you."

Eva's stomach gave another squeeze. She imagined what her mother's little something was. Plausibly a table full of food, fried and heavy.

"I'm not hungry, Mama. How long have they been gone?"

"Since about four-thirty. And of course you're hungry...."

Her mother's monologue went on, but Eva tuned out, not objecting when her mother started making the bed again. Her gaze flew to the bedside clock. It was after nine already. Her father and Adam had been gone for almost five hours. *Five hours.*

Eva briefly closed her eyes. Good Lord, five hours with Tolly Mavros could get a serial killer to admit where he'd hidden the bodies.

"They should be back in time for dinner at one," her mother said. "Come on, Eva, Yaya is probably wondering what's taking you so long."

Eva glimpsed a peek of something colorful in her mother's dress pocket. When Katina passed to make up the other side of the bed, Eva reached out and tugged on the piece of material.

A gentle swell of emotion swept through her—it was half of a crocheted baby bootie.

AN HOUR LATER, Eva felt ready to jump out of her skin. Not just because of the unbearable Louisiana heat. She had little choice but to deal with that. And forget that breakfast included her mother and grandmother and one of her aunts in the kitchen—where she slowly managed to put away a quarter of the meal Katina had prepared for her. And while no one remarked on their suspicions that she was pregnant, neither did they make a secret of the baby items all of them were knitting. And finally forget that she wanted to moan every time she got one of those smiles from her mother that said she was humoring her at the same time she made another loop with her crocheting needle, having graduated from booties to a receiving blanket.

Forget all that. *That* she could endure. The fact that Adam and her father had yet to come back, however, was another matter.

It wasn't so much what Adam might or might not do that concerned her. Since he didn't know anything about oystering, there was no possible way he could please her father. A factor that worked agreeably into her original plan. The problem was that her plans had altered since last night and Adam's absence threw a two-hundred-pound wrench into them. The plan now was to leave a.s.a.p. But she couldn't do that until he returned.

What information Adam might have spilled under her father's probing was something else she chose not to think about.

Needing to escape the kitchen and the conspiracy buzzing among the three well-meaning members of her family, Eva excused herself. She went upstairs, got her laptop and stole out the back door. The squeak of the springs then the gentle slap of the wooden screen door as it closed brought back memories that were both familiar and reassuring. She tightened her grip on the handle of the laptop, then stepped down the porch stairs, peering through the thick stand of Spanish moss–cloaked oaks and cypresses some fifty yards away. The hardwoods bordered the backyard and separated the house from her father's oystering dock and warehouse. She couldn't make out a thing past the lush vines twisted around the gnarled bark barrier.

She started in the direction of the hidden path that led to the dock, stopping restlessly, then starting again. She couldn't sit here all day. But she couldn't very well pack yet, either. She suspected if she did, she'd discover Yaya had unpacked again the minute her back was turned.

Eva pushed a slender, mossy oak branch out of the way and started along the path that stretched some twenty yards before she emerged on the other side and saw the bayou. Named Bayou Old Faithful, the slow-moving stream that, at this point, was as wide as a river, was one of many that snaked off Bayou Lafourche just off to her left where the dock was, and emptied into Timbalier Bay some six miles downstream.

What was Adam doing now? Did he take to heart what she had said last night about acting like a geek? Was he making her father dislike him? Or was her father seeing what *she* had glimpsed last night? That Adam was a good-natured man, with good genes, who would make a great son-in-law?

Eva stepped out from the stand of hardwoods. For a moment she stared at the large metal structure that served as both a warehouse and an office for her father's oystering business. It had been painted a soft blue since she'd been here last. She moved toward the gaping loading doors.

"Hey, Jimmy," she said, greeting the gangly young Cajun just inside. He was scrubbing down crude wooden tables and the concrete floor in preparation for the oysters her father would bring back.

"Hey, yourself, Eva." He leaned against the soapy, large-brushed broom and grinned at her from beneath a baseball cap that read Mavros Seafood. He shoved the hat back and drew his hand across his forehead. "Your father said something about the guy with him this morning being his son-in-law. I gathered you must be here, too. Welcome home."

Home. She tucked her hair behind her ear. "Did it look like Papa was going to give Adam a hard time?"

Jimmy's grin widened and his accent thickened. "The guy'll be lucky if Tolly doesn't throw him in the middle of a mud lump and just up and leave him there."

Eva imagined Adam standing in the middle of the equivalent of a northern sandbar. A mud lump was the sediment that swept down through the Mississippi, the rivers and bayous, then lumped near the mouth of the Gulf.

"Good." Eva glanced toward the closed office door, taking little notice of Jimmy's puzzled expression. "I thought I'd just go in and work on some of the accounts I brought with me. Do you mind?"

"Naw, go on ahead."

Eva did, stopping to skim an order on the clipboard hanging on the wall near the glass door. She quietly went into the office and flicked on the light.

"Nothing ever changes," she murmured.

She put her laptop down on a metal desk, then cleared a pile of receipts, work orders and a few uncashed checks off a ledger. She shook her head at her father's nearly illegible scrawls that stopped at a date weeks ago.

Eva swept her hair back from her face, then sank into the cracked leather chair she remembered from childhood. She put the receipts back down, then reached for her laptop and opened it up. She considered herself a good accountant, but not even she would attempt to make any sense out of her father's mess. Besides, she would need a lot longer than a couple of hours to do it.

Slipping the Honeycutt diskettes out of her dress pocket, she slid one into the disk drive and accessed the directory. Without delay, the file names popped up. She frowned, leaned closer and adjusted the brightness on the LCD screen. Most of the files bore sequential numbers...all except one. She selected the file then accessed the menu to open it.

The screen went instantly dark and a loud noise issued from the laptop's tiny speaker. She jumped, afraid she had crashed the drive. Reaching to reboot the system, she stopped when yellow graphic stars arced across the screen and a tinny, haunted type of music started playing.

That's odd.

Triumph of the Gladiators printed across the screen.

It's a game.

Eva accessed the menu system again and scanned the other files on the diskette, finding them all plainly related to the Honeycutt account. That's strange. Why would Oliver put a personal game on a working disk? She smiled, recalling that Oliver had always done curious little things like that.

Lifting her damp hair from her neck with one hand, she popped the diskette from the drive and slipped in the next one. She found the files she needed, tucked her hair into a loose twist, then got down to work.

A while later, her back started aching from spending so much time in the same position. She got up and stretched listlessly. Through the door window she saw

Jimmy was readying the machine that would divide the oysters into netted bags that held fifty pounds each and tag them. Eva turned back toward the desk, catching a glimpse of a picture frame peeking out from a pile of papers. She carefully slipped it out. Her heart gave a tender squeeze as she noticed it was a copy of her high-school graduation photo.

There was a tap at the door, then Jimmy opened it. "Eva, they're back."

Her misgivings—lost in the concentration of her chosen chore—returned. Especially because she knew Jimmy meant his words as a warning. Tolly Mavros didn't think his business was the place for any woman. Not even his daughter. Especially his daughter. No matter that she was a CPA and could help him with the mess he had created.

She slid her diskettes into her dress pocket, shut off her laptop and the light, then slipped through the door.

Out of the confines of the office, Eva heard the steady *put-put* of the boat engine on the river. She emerged from the warehouse and shaded her eyes from the powerful, hazy midday sun. In the cool dimness of the office, she hadn't noticed how hot and humid it had become. Now it hit her like a wet, sultry wave. She glanced at where her damp dress clung to her rear and legs from where she'd been sitting. Peeling the material away from her slick skin, she watched the boat pull up, *Eva II* stenciled in black across the bow, her father expertly maneuvering it through the dark green water into the slip. His flat, short-billed black cap prevented her from seeing much of his face as he concentrated on where he was going.

She sought Adam on the deck of the boat. He was nowhere to be found. Remembering Jimmy's earlier comment, she idly wondered if her father *had* left him on a mud lump.

Then she spotted him and the heat of the day was nothing compared to the heat that seared through her body.

Adam's sculpted, glistening upper torso was stripped bare, his brown polyester slacks riding low on his slim hips, giving her a tantalizing peek at the dark blond hair that trailed a line below his navel, then disappeared into his sweat-soaked pants. His feet were bare, and he'd rolled up the legs of his slacks to midcalf. Eva's mouth watered as she watched the muscles of his back work as he secured the back of the boat while her father saw to the front.

She swallowed hard. If Adam Gardner had intended to act like a nerd for her father's benefit, he had failed miserably.

Then he turned around. Even from that distance she could see his glasses were smudged and dirty, his face covered with soot from God only knew where. When he saw her standing with her arms crossed over her stomach, he started waving to her as if he were an overgrown kid returning from his first camping trip.

The grin that eased across her tense face was caused by relief and gratitude. There was no way her father could have taken to him.

Adam Gardner might be just the type of man the female Mavroses approved of, but Tolly would expect something far different than what Adam offered. There were to be no wimpy sons-in-law for this man. His definition of a true man would run somewhere along the lines of a gruff, foulmouthed oysterman like himself. Someone who would stand up for himself, stand up to him, take a stance that showed he had an ounce of passion in him.

Eva rested a hand against her damp neck, heated memories of the previous evening surging back to her.

Oh, Adam had passion all right. Just not the type her father could appreciate.

"Hi, Eva," Adam called to her, stepping off the boat onto the wooden dock.

"Hi, Adam," she called back softly.

A warm gulf breeze carried her father's murmured Greek curses to her ears and Eva wanted to smile. Urged on by more than gratitude, she strolled to the dock and to Adam's side, slipping her arm around his waist. A jolt of awareness spread over her from head to foot as her skin met his hot, hard body. She tried to pull away, but Adam's strong arm around her shoulders didn't allow her to.

She quietly cleared her throat. "Did you have fun?"

He grinned down at her, his gaze roving over her face. "Let's say this morning was very...enlightening."

Warmth pulsed through her and she pressed her lips to his neck, ceasing the instant she did so.

The movement came so naturally, so easily, she questioned her own sanity. He finally released his hold on her. She gently pulled away, licking the salty taste of him from her lips, her senses overwhelmed with emotions as foreign to her as the spark of spontaneity that had moved her to kiss him in the first place.

"Hi, Papa," she said as her father moved toward the dock side of the boat.

He murmured a greeting she couldn't quite make out, then asked what she was doing out there.

"Waiting for you and Adam, of course," she said, giving herself points for not asking him where he expected her to be. She didn't need to ask. She already knew. In Tolly's eyes, Eva's place was back at the house, helping her mother prepare the afternoon meal.

Her father hmmphed his response, and every remarkable, wonderful emotion within Eva wilted.

She told herself she was being childish. That her

need for her father's affection was something that she should have gotten over years ago...back when she finally figured out she might never get it. Still, she wished just once he would express himself in a way that didn't make her feel she was one huge disappointment. While a competent cook, she shied away from it, mainly because it was expected of her. She had, however, always yearned to go oystering. It had long proven a sore spot that while her name might be on the boat, she wasn't welcome on it.

"The morning's not done yet, Adam," her father said, rocking a pulley toward him.

"Yes, right, of course."

Looking all the world like a man ready to please, Adam reboarded the boat and awkwardly offered his help. The relief Eva felt earlier melted into something else entirely. It took her a second to realize it was envy. Not of her father's brusque treatment of Adam. But that Tolly Mavros would even take the time to tell him how to do something the right way. It's something he'd never done with her.

Eva slowly walked back along the dock. For the first time, she noticed her brother, Pete, leaning against the warehouse. Given the sober expression on his face, she wasn't the only one who felt left out. Which was odd, because she had always been envious of Pete's relationship with her father. She didn't like to admit that she'd ever been jealous of her brother. In some ways he'd had it harder than she had, having to be at Papa's beck and call since he was old enough to walk. When he had matured, he had developed his own dreams, his own interests. Discovered he had a passion for building boats rather than using them to fish. But Tolly Mavros wouldn't hear of Pete veering away from family tradition. Every Mavros male had been a fisherman and his son would continue the legacy. End of discussion.

Pete glanced at Eva. Their gazes locked for a long moment. She started in his direction, to tell him she knew what he was feeling, that she'd felt the same way when Papa had lavished all his attention on him. But he turned from her and drifted into the warehouse where he would presumably help with the bagging.

ADAM GLANCED at Eva where she stood off to the side of the hulking warehouse. The hem of her flowered dress skimmed the middle of her toned, tanned thighs. Her hair was a dark, wild mass that somehow made her eyes look bigger, making her whole presence that much more distracting.

Back there, when Tolly was bringing the boat in, he had spotted Eva, and a soft humming had drifted through his body. A humming whose origin came not from the vibration of the boat engine, but instead as a reaction to the captivating woman waiting for him. In that one moment, it was easy to imagine her one of Odysseus's sirens and that it was her silent, haunted song that hummed through him. That it was for her song alone that he was returning to shore.

Now Adam dragged the back of his hand across his wet forehead and followed Pete's lead by spreading the oysters out on the table. He needed to get out of there, out of Louisiana and back to some semblance of reality, quick. He fully intended to make Eva stick to her promise that they'd stay for only one day.

The woman offered a fathomless wealth of contradictions. Hell, his own emotions were a bit on the contradictory side when it came to Eva Mavros Burgess. After she'd shared her condition the night before, the last thing he should be thinking about was how sexy she looked, and how hard it had been to lie next to her all night and not follow through with what had started with that kiss. But when she had slipped her slender arm around his waist on the dock, then pressed her mouth against his neck, he had battled against the need to claim those provocative lips in a kiss that would surpass a friendly greeting. What stopped him was the shadow in Eva's eyes when she spoke to her father.

Looking at the older man now, Adam decided that Tolly Mavros had to be one of the most direct people he had ever met. When he'd awakened to a rough squeeze on the shoulder early that morning, he had started, thinking it was Eva, having changed her mind about his sleeping in the bed. Instead, he'd made out the outline of Tolly's uniquely carved face inches away from his and couldn't for the life of him think what Eva's father wanted. He didn't find out until after hastily dressing and meeting him in the hall where Tolly had said they were going oystering.

Oystering, for God's sake.

Until that point, the only things Adam knew about oysters were that they were supposed to be an aphrodisiac, they were expensive and you didn't prepare them at home unless you knew where they came from. Of course, he had never stopped to think about how they were actually dredged up. But Tolly apparently had been dead set on showing him. Something that caught Adam off guard because aside from commenting on his hair, Eva's father hadn't spoken a word to him.

And two hours into the already sweltering day, when the sun had finally started to rise over the river and countless bayous like a fiery orange, Adam had been convinced Tolly might never utter another word to him again.

The first half of the trip was spent in silence—aside

from terse orders from his temporary father-in-law. Awkward silences that stopped being so awkward when Adam figured out Tolly wasn't much of a talker. It wasn't that he wasn't interested. He just honestly didn't have anything to say. Adam mopped the sweat from his forehead again. But when Tolly Mavros did have something to say, he could be as jovial as a comic, or as tenacious as a pit bull with a rabbit clenched in his jaws. It depended on what his mind was on.

Of course, Adam hadn't forgotten Eva's request from the night before: he was to do everything he could to make her father not like him. And he had. From jamming the controls for the dredger so it got stuck in the upright position, to "accidentally" dumping a couple dozen or so oysters back into the water. He had gone out of his way to come off, if not as a complete imbecile, then as a top contender. He'd earned more than a few tirades of guttural words he hadn't understood. But there had been one word he did understand. It came after he had maneuvered the dredger and dumped its contents directly in the spot Eva's father had indicated. Tolly had slapped him on the back hard enough to dislodge half a digested steak then heartily said, "Bravo."

Adam rubbed the back of his neck, wishing he hadn't purposely smudged his fake glasses, then went back to helping bag the last of the oysters. It was funny, but that one word coming from Tolly Mavros had made him grin.

Finally, Tolly announced the morning's work done and Adam stepped up next to where Eva watched nearby. She looked more fresh and appealing than any one woman had the right to look. And made Adam feel that much grimier. Lord, but he felt as if he'd just returned from a month-long tour of hard labor.

"Here, let me clean those for you," she said, reaching up to take the glasses from his face.

Adam caught her wrist before she could slip them all the way off, feeling the leap of her pulse beneath his thumb, then slid that same thumb up and down the underside of her wrist.

"Thanks, but I can get them," he said, his exhaustion chased away by a rush of desire for the woman in front of him. A woman as earthy as the rich soil that banked the bayous, and more alluring than an enchantress in an erotic novel. A woman he needed to stay well away from.

The expression on her face mirrored the one she wore after talking to Tolly. Disappointment. It bothered Adam more than he cared to admit. So much so, he released her hand then took off his glasses himself, offering them to her. Surely, he could let her clean his glasses without succumbing to the overwhelming urge to take her to bed.

"Be careful," he said, dropping his gaze when she looked at him closely…too closely. "They scratch easy."

He caught her brief smile. "I'll be careful."

She walked toward the back of the warehouse. He watched her go, glad for once that he didn't have to do it through the thick lenses. God, but that woman had a walk on her. And the way her summery dress drifted around her thighs made him want to groan.

He had to get out of there.

"Come." Tolly hit him on the back so hard he nearly choked. "We wash up outside. You're hungry, no?"

"Yes," Adam said, allowing the shorter, stockier man to lead him out of the dim warehouse. "Hungry."

He didn't think Tolly would be happy to learn what exactly he was hungry for. Especially since he wasn't the man Tolly thought him to be.

"NO, MAMA, we have to go," Eva said across the dinner table. She gently waved her grandmother away from where she tried to hand her a slice of fresh bread. "It's a long drive, and we both have to be back at work Tuesday morning."

"But that's ridiculous. We haven't seen you for over a year, Eva. And we've only just met Adam. Certainly, you can stay at least through tomorrow and spend Labor Day with us." Katina reached out to place her hand on Adam's arm where he sat next to her. "Tell her, Adam. Tell my stubborn daughter that you must stay."

Eva's gaze shifted to Adam's face. She hoped that Adam would back her up this time. She really needed him to.

Eva's brother, Pete, dropped his fork to his plate. "Leave them be, Mama. If Eva says they have to go, then they have to go. God, does everything have to be a battle around here?"

An uncomfortable silence punctuated by the whirl of the ceiling fan followed Pete's statement. Eva watched her brother in quiet sympathy. *He feels threatened by Adam's presence,* she realized. Did he think his position as the only son was in jeopardy now that another man had shown up? Or was he thinking about all he, himself, had given up without a fight?

This made Eva feel even guiltier about her deception. Bill would have never made Pete feel insecure, because Bill would never have come down here.

She dropped her gaze, wishing the heat didn't make her feel so listless.

"Sorry, Mrs. Mavros," Adam said quietly. "But Eva's right." He met her gaze meaningfully. "We really do have to get back."

Those at the table remained silent. Eva tamped down a comment about how none of her objections were taken seriously, while Adam said one sentence and it was accepted as a fact.

Sluggishly stabbing a piece of fried zucchini, she sensed her father's gaze on her.

"Your mother is right. You should stay," he said. Then more quietly, he added, "I'd like you to stay."

Eva shifted her gaze to his face, but he had gone back to eating. She wondered if she had heard his last comment at all.

The tension at the table for the remainder of the midday meal settled into Eva's stomach like a tight knot. She was relieved when she could finally excuse herself, the key to the guest bedroom tucked safely in her dress pocket. Earlier, during a rare moment alone, she'd sneaked into the pantry and went through a metal box that held copies of all the house's keys. She intended to make up the guest bedroom for Adam and let him lie down there while she rested in her old room before making the drive to Jersey.

Collecting her laptop from where she'd left it in the kitchen, she climbed the stairs, wondering if Adam would still want to stop in New Orleans on the way back up. At this point, she wasn't sure if she was up to showing him the sights she had promised. All she wanted to do was crawl into her wicker bed at home with the remote, a jar of chunky peanut putter, a bowl of celery sticks, set the air-conditioner to full blast and forget this whole weekend ever happened. Maybe then she could concentrate on her life—and the life of her baby—again, without having to worry about her strained relationship with her father. And she'd be able to forget about her lustful thoughts for Adam.

Eva paused at the top of the steps and leaned briefly against the hall wall. Her reason for coming back hadn't been solely to prepare her father for her divorce. She had wanted to mend the damaged relationship.

Repair it before the truth about her most recent failure caused the rift between them to grow wider. She needed to strengthen a generation of weak family ties for the sake of the baby growing within her.

Pushing off the wall, she picked up her step, telling herself it didn't matter now. In a couple of hours she and Adam would be on the road, and everything would be back to the way it was before they'd come.

Intending to unlock the guest room through the connecting bathroom, she opened her bedroom door and slipped in. She took three steps then came to a complete stop. She stood in the middle of a circle of clothes she recognized as a combination of hers and Adam's.

It took a second to sink in that what she was seeing wasn't normal. That the dresser drawers tilting out at odd angles, the uneven mattresses, and the contents of the closet covering the floor weren't a result of spring-cleaning—or another of her grandmother's attempts to get them to stay. The room had been trashed.

7

DOWNSTAIRS, the alarm in Eva's voice as she called for him sent a tidal wave of panic through Adam's veins. Pushing away from the dinner table, he met the gazes of her brother and father, then rushed from the room. He didn't stop until he found Eva, safe, in her bedroom.

"Are you all right?" He gently grasped her arms and pulled her to him.

"I'm—I'm fine," she said.

Her face was a little too pale, her skin too cool beneath his fingers.

Beyond the relief upon seeing she was okay came the disturbing awareness that somebody had rifled through the room. And had done a fine job of it, too. When Tolly caught up with him, Adam stepped aside to let him enter the room.

"Are you okay?" Tolly asked gruffly.

Eva nodded, her hand shaking as she pushed her hair back from her face. "The room was like this when I came in."

"There's been a break-in," Adam said tightly.

Stepping past Eva, he checked the bathroom and the closet. Then he moved into the hall, doing a quick search of the other rooms to make sure the intruder wasn't still lurking somewhere inside the house. He wasn't surprised that the only room that had been touched was Eva's.

Damn. Between his baffling feelings for Eva, and

balancing the dual roles he was playing as an under cover agent *and* as Eva's husband, he'd let himself ge sucked into a false sense of security. Allowed himsel to believe that the thirteen hundred miles betweer Belle Rivage and Edison, New Jersey, was enough tc erase any potential danger.

The Ford. The guy who had broken into Eva's car Adam had suspected all along it had been more than a random act. Now he knew. He and Eva had been fol lowed.

He walked back into Eva's bedroom. She and her fa ther were talking in hushed tones, and she had he arms squeezed protectively around her stomach. Tolly had moved farther into the room and had a bunchec towel clenched in his right hand. He picked somethin; up off the dresser with his other hand, then put i slowly back down.

Eva's face paled and she glanced to Adam. He nod ded, indicating the rest of the rooms were untouched.

"What is going on here?" Tolly demanded of Adam

"I don't know beyond what we all see." Which wa accurate if you relied on the surface truth. And righ now, Adam decided that's all that mattered. At least a far as Eva's family was concerned.

"You don't know." Tolly's response was tense as h eyed the things around him with disdain. His thick fin gers clenched around the towel he held.

Adam cleared his throat. "Did anybody see any thing suspicious? Anyone strange hanging around?"

He looked at Eva's mother, grandmother and brother where they now stood in the hall.

"Mama and I were in the kitchen all morning," Ka tina said quietly.

Adam looked to Pete. "I left early and didn't returr until about an hour ago. I didn't see anything," Pet answered.

Swearing silently, Adam turned back to Eva and Tolly, but neither paid much attention to him.

"Somebody should call the police," Adam said.

Pete quietly left, apparently to do as he'd requested.

Adam thrust his hand through his hair. He needed to call Weckworth and tell him what was going on. To see if there had been any other developments in the case his boss had neglected to tell him about.

But right now, he needed to make sure Eva was all right. She turned from where she leaned against one of the wrought-iron bedposts and her face went even paler. Frowning, Adam followed her gaze to her father's feet. He moved closer and understood Eva's fear. Tolly stood on her divorce papers.

Eva's gaze fastened on Adam's face, her expression alarmed, her eyes pleading with him to do something, anything, to keep her father from seeing the documents.

"Tolly, you're upset," Adam said, slapping his back as Tolly had done to him that morning. "Why don't you go wait downstairs for the police? There's nothing you can do in here now."

Tolly looked at the items littering the floor. Eva rushed forward.

"Adam's right, Papa," she said, stepping close enough to force his attention to her rather than the papers he stood on. A light sheen of perspiration glistened on her tanned skin. "Go now and let me and Adam check to see if anything's missing."

Muttering what Adam guessed were Greek curses, Tolly let Adam guide him toward the door. Eva's mother and grandmother took over from there.

As soon as the trio was halfway down the hall, Adam quietly closed the door and faced Eva. She was plucking the papers from the carpet, smoothing them out with trembling hands.

"Planning to get married again, Eva? Or do you a[l]ways carry your divorce papers with you? You know in case you need them for identification purposes?" h[e] asked dryly, seeking out his briefcase in the mess su[r]rounding them.

"After I found I was pregnant...and I agreed to l[et] Bill out of our marriage..." Eva faltered, apparent[ly] trying to slow her words. "Everything happened [so] fast. I mean, I knew it was going to happen, I just did[n't] expect his attorneys to be so successful in the exped[i]tion of the process...." She closed her eyes and drew [a] deep, shaky breath. "I'm rambling. What it com[es] down to is I got the final papers Thursday and, wel[l] didn't have a chance to take them out of my attac[hé] case."

Adam hadn't realized her divorce from Bill Burges[s] had been *that* recent. But it didn't take a genius to d[o] the math. While two months was an extraordinari[ly] short amount of time to obtain a divorce decree, wit[h] the right connections and without contest it wasn't im[-]possible. He shoved his fingers through his hair agai[n] cursing the heat, and damning the twist in circum[-]stances. He bent to rummage around the clothes pil[e] outside the closet door. It was there he found his brie[f]case...open.

Empty.

His pulse rate vaulted. He tore through the plasti[c] protected clothes on the floor. He stopped after he'[d] combed them a second time. There was no mistak[e] about it. The intruder may or may not have found wh[at] he was looking for. But he had walked away with on[e] important thing: Adam's 9 mm pistol.

"Damn, damn, damn," he muttered, stepping to th[e] window. A police car pulled into the driveway. Ye[s] the officers would expect a complete report on wh[at] was missing. No, Adam wouldn't mention a wor[d] about his gun. Not now. Not when this case had taken such a sharp turn.

Another thing Adam knew was that he and Eva weren't going anywhere, whether they liked it or not. Since the danger had started in Belle Rivage, it must end here, as well.

His biggest problem lay in how he was going to continue to act like a nerd and still manage to get answers to some very important questions.

Number one being whether or not Eva Mavros Burgess was involved in the illegal scheme with her boss, Norman Sheffert.

EVA COULDN'T REMEMBER a time when she felt more spent, more violated, more out of sorts than she did at that moment. That included the day two months ago when she returned home from work to an empty house. Bill had taken every piece of furniture, each plate and glass, all the linens, even the CD collection, leaving only those items she had brought into their marriage. She remembered thinking he must have had two trucks and ten movers to have accomplished the feat in so short a time. She had also been struck with the numbing sensation that it was truly over between them. He had destroyed everything they had ever shared with that one, heartless act.

Now, sitting at her family's dining-room table in Belle Rivage—a half hour after the local police had taken their statements—Eva rested the fingers of her right hand against her stiff, clammy neck and stared at the Greek coffee in a tiny cup near her left wrist. The late-afternoon sun slanted in through the lacy curtains, making odd, shifting patterns on the surface of the table and increasing the almost unbearable heat of the room.

"You *must* stay now," her father said from the end of the table.

Stay? As in forever? Eva sought out his gaze, but could read nothing in his expression except a challenge for her to object.

"He's right," Adam said where he sat next to her. "We should stay."

Eva fastened her gaze on him.

"At least until tomorrow morning, when things have had a chance to settle down." He pushed up his glasses, but Eva found the would-be nervous action somehow incongruous with his firm words.

"Adam, *sweetheart*," she said, her throat thick, her muscles taut. "You know we have to get back to Jersey. We're both behind in our work—"

"We can always see to our work from here. At least for a short time."

She blinked slowly several times, not quite buying his innocent expression. Not when there was a tension around his provocative mouth that warranted further examination.

"We can always download the files we need from Alice first thing Tuesday morning," he said.

Tuesday? How did they get from leaving a.s.a.p. to getting their files via modem from Sheffert, Logan and Brace Tuesday morning?

Eva pressed her fingertips against her forehead.

"Good, then it's settled," her father stated, rising from the table.

He didn't say anything else, merely left the room. Eva didn't need to ask where he was going. Greek custom included taking a siesta in the afternoons right after dinner.

"Your room's all straightened." Eva looked up to where her grandmother had rejoined them. Eva had assumed she had gone up for her own siesta. Obviously, she'd assumed wrong.

Eva sighed. "Yaya, you shouldn't have done that." Didn't anyone think she could take care of herself? She'd lived in New Jersey for years on her own. Who did they think made her bed there? Cleaned up after her? Told her when and what to eat?

She knew her vexation was due more to frustration, and that her grandmother was just trying to be helpful, but her irrational emotions refused to go away. Emotionally and physically spent, she pushed away from the table and headed upstairs where she hoped everything would look a lot better after some rest.

"YOUR COVER is blown, Grayson. It's as simple as that," FBI Deputy Chief John Weckworth said.

Adam tightened his fingers against the wallet-size cellular phone that had gone untouched in a narrow false bottom of his briefcase. He bit back a curse, telling himself that nothing was simple. Not anymore. Not since somebody had gone through Eva's room and his gun had come up missing.

After making sure Eva was sleeping, Adam had ducked into the guest room next door where he had placed the call to his superior. He'd brought Eva's laptop computer with him and it sat on a nearby dresser. He glanced at the closed door to the bathroom, envisioning Eva lying in that sinfully sumptuous bed just a few yards and two walls away.

"My gut tells me you're wrong, John." He crossed to the computer. "What happened today has nothing to do with me or my cover."

There was a brief silence as he opened the laptop.

"Then that means Eva Burgess was the target," Weckworth said, putting into words his own thoughts.

"Maybe."

Weckworth cursed. "Tell me, Grayson, if you and Burgess aren't the targets, who is? The fisherman? Oh, wait, let me guess. It's the little old lady."

Adam gave a wry smile at the reference to Eva's grandmother. "Actually, I'm thinking that someone isn't the target at all, but *something* is."

There was another silence, then Weckworth muttered something and put him on hold.

Adam hadn't told his superior about his missing gun, and was relieved he hadn't. He could imagine what sarcasm he would have suffered through had he given Weckworth that piece of ammunition.

He *had* told him about the guy who broke into Eva's car, and gave a detailed description of the Ford he'd been driving. Adam hadn't spotted the car or the guy since, but that meant little other than the man had let his guard down. He knew instinctively that the two incidents were connected and that led to his theory that the intruder was after something....

Adam stared down at the open laptop to find folded sheets of paper lying across the keyboard. He picked them up. They were Eva's divorce papers. She must have stuck them in there after the close call with her father.

"I'm back," Weckworth said.

"Good thing. I was just about to hang up on you." Adam glanced at the still-closed door. "To return to what I was saying, I don't think what the intruder was after is so much the question here as the identity of the culprit himself. Or herself." He frowned. Until he had proof one way or the other, he couldn't completely rule out Eva as a suspect.

"Any theories?" Weckworth asked.

"A couple. But they're not at the sharing stage yet. What about you?"

"The same."

Adam dragged in a breath of the hot, humid air, then looked back down at the divorce papers in his right hand. With a flick of a finger, he turned to the second page of the stamped document. Past the official recognition of the filer and respondent—the filer being one pond scum William B. Burgess.

"Get somebody from the New Orleans office out here," he muttered to Weckworth. "I don't care who. I can't stay in character and insist on staying around the house twenty-four hours a day."

"Two guys are already on their way," Weckworth said, giving him another cell phone number. "You're not the only one with gut instincts, you know. Call me later to let me know if you find anything on that laptop."

Adam broke the connection then called the number of the agents en route and arranged a brief meeting with them in an hour, near the warehouse. Afterward he dropped the cell phone to the dresser and turned to the next page of the divorce papers. A dark expression spread over his face.

Bill Burgess had signed away all parental rights to his child.

The baby Eva carried.

And all indications were that he'd not only done it voluntarily, he'd insisted on it.

Cursing, Adam tossed the papers to the dresser, then sat in front of the laptop computer, determined to break this case one way or another. And even more resolved to put his growing feelings for the woman in the next room out of his mind. Both for her safety...and his own.

EVA AWAKENED from her nap to the sound of a car horn. Pushing upright on the still-made bed, she saw her room was nearly pitch-black but for a purplish haze. Bewildered, she climbed from the bed and peeked through the window where she saw her aunt and uncle getting out of their Honda. The warm greeting from her father downstairs baffled her further as she turned to look at the bedside clock. It read eight-thirty.

She had slept for five straight hours.

Adam.

A glance told her he had not slept on the other side of the bed. She moved toward the bathroom and the door to the guest room. He wasn't there and hadn't slept on that bed, either. She returned to her own bedroom and noticed her laptop was gone. Adam must have taken it downstairs.

Pushing her tangled hair back from her face, she switched on the lights and lethargically got herself together.

Minutes later, she walked into the dining room to find it empty. She followed the sound of the voices through the living room and halted at the doors to the screened-in side porch that offered a captivating view of the sunset. She had stepped right into another family gathering. But this time, a thorough, lingering glance told her that her father was actually smiling. Well, he was doing the Tolly Mavros equivalent to smiling, anyway, which was a wry, sardonic slight upturn to his full mouth as he filled a wineglass for her uncle. Tolly's upbeat mood was better displayed by his gregarious bursts of conversation and his frequent prompting of his guests to eat or drink, or both.

"You're up," her mother greeted Eva, spotting her.

Eva frowned when she saw that Adam held the prominent position next to her father. He sat in a chair usually reserved for her brother, Pete, who was noticeably absent. Adam smiled at her in a modest way that came off as somehow *too* innocent, *too* vague, and all *too* provocative. Her grandmother pulled out the chair between her and Adam. Eva hesitantly went to it. She should have given herself more time to wake up, to gather her thoughts together.

She sat down and noticed that Yaya was slipping something into a white plastic bag. Eva captured the scrap of material, finding it to be a continuation of the pink, blue and white blanket her grandmother had been working on earlier in the day.

"Yaya—"

"Eat, Eva, eat," her grandmother urged, pushing a full plate in front of her.

Eva clutched the bag and the blanket in it, then stuffed both under her chair, out of her grandmother's reach. The white-haired woman merely smiled and filled a glass with milk for her.

Eva turned toward Adam and he winked at her. An ardent flush swept across her skin and she shifted her gaze to her plate. It was piled high with seafood.

"You're going to have to tell them soon, Eva," Adam murmured, his breath stirring the hair over her left ear.

She shivered, not sure what bothered her more. The way he insisted on using the Greek pronunciation of her name, or the electric way she reacted to him.

"Did you do this?" she whispered, gesturing toward her plate.

His smile told her he had.

She picked up the plate and used her fork to carefully transfer the oysters, shrimp and lobster on top of his already generous helpings.

"I'm allergic to shellfish," she said quietly, hoping her father wouldn't overhear.

Adam's eyebrows lifted above the rim of his glasses, his gaze probing and intimate.

Eva wasn't sure she was comfortable with the perusal. Adam Gardner was coming to know more about her than anyone else ever had. Including Bill. She grimaced. Especially Bill.

"Here," her grandmother said on the other side of her. "Have some fish."

Eva raised her hand to protest the healthy helping, then she slumped back in her chair. Just because the scaly thing was on her plate didn't mean she had to eat it.

The atmosphere around the table was much different from the night before. Eva guessed it might be because they were outside but suspected it had more to do with her father's open participation tonight. She glanced at him, noticing his cheeks were flushed with color, his dark eyes sparkling with mischief in the light from the three gas lanterns on the table. Apparently his appetite had returned to normal as well, evidenced by the way he lifted another oyster on a half shell to his mouth.

"Is everything all right?" Adam murmured.

Eva realized she had sighed. She glanced at him. "Sure, I'm fine."

"So, Adam," Eva's Uncle Theo asked from across the table. "You haven't told us yet how you met our Eva."

Eva's gaze still resting on his face, she lifted an eyebrow, hoping he remembered what she had told him. But when she saw a devilish gleam in his brown eyes, her heart surged into her throat. She anchored her hand to his thigh under the table and squeezed to let him know she would handle this.

"At work. We met at work," she said quickly, nearly knocking over her glass of milk as she reached for it with her other hand. "I was working on his business accounts. Two years ago this January, in fact."

Her uncle grinned. "Two years, huh? You must be a fast worker to have gotten Eva to marry you so quickly."

Eva's father hmmphed, but everyone seemed to ignore him. Everyone but Eva.

"You know how true love goes," Adam said smoothly. Too smoothly. Eva studied him, trying to ignore the way he had trapped her hand against his thigh...ignoring the way his thumb scraped against her palm. "I knew the moment I laid eyes on her that she would be the woman I'd spend the rest of my life with."

Something within Eva went soft. Adam turned toward her, his eyes holding a curious shadow she couldn't quite define. An honesty that made her heartbeat speed up, her stomach flutter and her knees squeeze tightly together.

She urged her gaze away, telling herself she was being ridiculous. Adam had made that part up to convince her family that their fake courtship had been natural. But the way she felt now was far from natural. Not considering that the man sitting next to her was not her husband, and they had never gone out on a date, much less courted each other.

He tried to release her hand. She found herself preventing the move, clasping his fingers tighter as she forked her red snapper.

"And the wedding?" Eva's mother asked from the other end of the table.

Eva swallowed. Why was her mother doing this? She'd told her everything the day after the ceremony. "Bill and I went to the county courthouse. A judge performed the ceremony."

Her father stared at her as if she'd grown a second head. It wasn't until then that Eva realized she'd said "Bill."

Adam cleared his throat and tightened his hold on her hand. "Eva often calls me Bill since that's how most of my friends refer to me."

There were several nods, and quiet exchanges as the meal continued.

"Then you're not married in the eyes of the Church."

Eva wasn't surprised by her father's blunt statement. Her cheeks burned under his scrutiny.

"And if you're not married in the eyes of the Church, you're not married in the eyes of God." He pointed a finger toward the darkening sky.

Eva rested her head against her other hand, not up to an argument. Not tonight. Not after all that had happened in the past two days. Lingering in her mind was the question of what her father would do if he knew she and Adam were sharing a room in his house, but weren't married in anybody's eyes, much less God's.

"Actually, we've talked about that," Adam said, picking up the conversation. Eva jerked involuntarily, pulling his hand from his thigh to hers under the table. The back of his fingers caused tremors of sensation as they rasped against her knee. Eva nearly jumped, the warmth in her belly seeping lower. "We were thinking about arranging a church ceremony."

Eva focused on his face, battling between the erotic awareness caused by the innocent touch of his hand and the baffling comments coming from his all-too tempting mouth.

"Not now, but at some point soon," Adam clarified.

Inexplicably hungry for more than the food on her plate, she released her grip and urged his palm down against her bare knee. The forbidden heat of his skin chased the breath from her lungs, seeming to manipulate strings attached to her heart. She'd had a scare this afternoon, slept far longer than she had intended, and was facing her father's disapproval. Despite all that, Adam's command of the conversation brought her a measure of comfort…while her command of his hand

under the table caused a restlessness that had more to
do with sensual need than difficult questions.

"Oh, how wonderful," Katina said. "You must have
the ceremony down here. You know, so family can at-
tend."

Adam glanced at Eva, his expression telling her he
knew exactly what she was doing as she slowly urged
his fingers higher on her fevered skin. The contrast between his awkwardly reluctant participation in their
kiss the night before, and his hesitant yet willing participation as he touched her now threatened to make
her head spin. But she refused to continue to seek answers to questions that might not have any answers.
She was tired of trying to figure out the enigmatic man
next to her. In that one moment, she resolved to give
herself over to the wonderfully feminine and desirable
way he made her feel instead.

Lured by the safety of their under-table play, Eva
uncrossed her legs and scooted a little closer to the table, making sure the long, white tablecloth concealed
her secret activities. She was pleased by the surprise
that marked Adam's handsome face.

"Uh, yes," she said softly to her mother's suggestion
that they have the church ceremony in Louisiana. "We
might consider doing it—down here."

Eva had only the faintest notion of what she had
agreed to. All she could concentrate on was the hand
that had stopped maddeningly on her thigh. Adam
stabbed an oyster with his other hand and lifted it to
his mouth. She watched the action with rapt attention,
opening her mouth as if she were going to take in the
salty morsel. She wished for the first time in her life she
didn't break out in hives just smelling the shellfish.
Most people believed the oyster an aphrodisiac. Raised
in Louisiana, Eva knew the rumor to be a fact. Eating
the molluscan shellfish increased the blood's level of

zinc, thus elevating testosterone levels in men. S
every time Adam slipped one more oyster into his
mouth, he was promising that the next time they were
alone together, it would be harder for him—and her—
to pull away.

Forcing herself to pretend at least a passing interes
in the meal, Eva tried to concentrate on her own
plate...and nearly choked when Adam's hidden hand
drifted farther up between her legs and grazed the
thin, damp material of her panties. Liquid fire erupted
throughout her limbs. He took in her surprise and be
gan moving his hand away. She just barely stopped
herself from yelling no and trapped his hand where i
was, shamelessly pressing her hips against the thumb
that rested against her exquisite pressure point.

Her cheeks ablaze, she glanced around the table
smiling at her aunt when she caught her gaze. She
turned back to Adam, drinking in the curiously wicked
gleam in his eyes. Embarrassment swept through Eva
But mingling with it was a provocative allure that no
one knew exactly where Adam's hand was. They had
no idea that even now the pad of his thumb outlined
the edge of her panties, guided by her own hand
They'd never guess that he was slipping that same
thumb in—

"Tell us a little about yourself, Adam," her aunt said

The air rushed from Eva's lungs as the tip of his fin
ger brushed maddeningly against her pubic hair. He
knee jerked against the table and the contents tottere
She shuddered in near climax and quickly thrust h
hand back to the safety of his own thigh.

Adam's hoarse chuckle swept over her. Eva quietl
groaned, both in longing and in horror at her own bra
zen behavior.

"Oh, I don't think you'd be interested in hearin

about me," he responded. "My life is one long boring story."

"Are you from New Jersey?" Eva's cousin asked, ignoring his evasion.

Still, Adam's hand remained under the table and the temptation to guide those strong, long fingers back... Eva swallowed hard and searched his profile. She tried to quash the sensations clamoring for release, but was slowly coming to understand that ever since their not-so-innocent kiss the night before, she might never get rid of the hunger growing inside her, her craving for a man who was an awkward, charming nerd one minute, then a rakishly handsome, almost seductive rogue the next. The longing to know as much about the man as he was coming to know about her. She cleared her throat and trailed her hand down the cold side of her milk glass, restraining herself from acting on needs better ignored.

She couldn't exactly *ask* Adam about his past. Not in present company. But that didn't mean she couldn't listen.

"No, I'm not from Jersey. I'm from a small town in Ohio outside Toledo," he said quietly, his gaze trained on his food. He used the hand that had intimately touched her moments before to push up his glasses.

"How did you end up on the coast then?" her mother asked.

"I...relocated for career reasons."

Eva's eyebrows drew together. She watched the lean-fingered hand he rested on top of the table with fascination. Business reasons? One didn't decide to move halfway across the country to get an entry-level job at an accounting firm.

"Yes, I suppose you can't do much stock trading in Ohio," Eva's uncle said.

Bill was the stockbroker. Of course, Eva thought, Adam was playing the role they'd agreed on.

Adam laughed and nodded, but Eva saw the tension in his jaw.

"What about your family?"

"My family?" Adam repeated.

Eva's cousin smiled. "Certainly you have one."

Adam put down his fork and stiffened in his chair. "Actually, no, I don't," he said quietly. "My mother...my birth mother gave me up to the state when I was three. I never knew who my father was."

Eva reached out and lay her hand against his thigh. Not to restrain him. Not to incite passion. But for reasons that had nothing to do with either. She wanted to comfort him, let him know she felt more than sympathy, that she cared.

Adam glanced at her. Eva saw that telling her family just this little bit had cost him a lot. She also suspected he hadn't said it solely for their sakes. The intense look in his eyes told her the open, casual format of the conversation had allowed him a way to open up to her. And he now watched her for her response.

She gave it to him by way of a squeeze of his thigh and surprised even herself when she leaned over and spontaneously pressed her lips against his clean-shaven cheek.

When she slowly pulled back, Adam laughed and pushed up his glasses again. "I told you it was a long, boring story."

The awkward statement brought caring protests from those around the table, but thankfully, the moment proved to be the impetus to urge the conversation back to lighter territory. Under her hand, Eva felt Adam's hard muscles relax.

Much later, the informal get-together broke up and the women began clearing the table. As Eva slowly stacked plates and gathered glasses, she realized her movements were jerky and nervous, the need to be alone with Adam her primary focus.

"Leave them," her grandmother said, touching her arm. "We can take care of the dishes."

Eva nudged her hand away. "I can help, Yaya."

"Better you should show your sweet Adam your moon down on the bayou, no?"

My moon. Eva gave a little smile. In her early teens, she used to sneak out of the house in the middle of the night and steal down to the dock, spending long hours telling her dreams to the moon. Once, her grandmother had secretly followed her, obviously out of concern, but said nothing when Eva had sneaked back into the house just minutes before her father would rise to go oystering. Yaya had been sitting in the kitchen, giving her a conspiratorial smile as Eva hurried past her to make her way back upstairs.

Funny how she forgot things like that in the harsh, rational light of adulthood. Funny how merely remembering it brought back a swell of nostalgia. And a desire to show Adam her moon.

Giving her grandmother a kiss on the cheek, Eva threaded her fingers through Adam's and tugged him to his feet.

"Go, go," Yaya said when he hesitated.

Eva gave him a glance that told him to come.

8

THE DEWY GRASS was soft under their feet as they walked, the fragrance of nearby jasmine intoxicating. Adam glanced toward the trees and underbrush that bordered the property. On his order, the two agents he'd met up with outside the warehouse should be constantly skirting the place, on the lookout for anything suspicious. He knew that the evening's visitors would make it difficult for the agents, but he'd had no control over that. What he could do was make sure that if the house was being watched, the watcher would be spotted. His first concern was keeping Eva and her family safe. Coming in a very close second was solving this case, no matter the consequences.

And the urgency of both objectives grew with each moment that ticked by.

He'd broken Eva's password code on her laptop and found nothing of use on the hard drive. Nothing but legitimate accounts and postings. Neither had a search of her purse turned up any sign of the Honeycutt diskettes. And there were no unusual deposits listed in her checkbook register. No suspicious names in her address book. Nothing that tied her to anything that was happening. Which was the source of tremendous relief…and worry. If she wasn't involved, what did she have that someone wanted? And could he find it before that someone did?

Adam shifted his gaze to where his fingers were still laced with Eva's. He wondered at the feeling that pulsed beneath the wary tension that filled him. The undefined emotion had less to do with sex and more with the woman who walked next to him. He had never said to anyone what he had told Eva's family earlier that evening. And while it wasn't the entire reason he turned love and commitment away, what he had experienced at revealing the little he had was oddly cathartic. A relief and a reassurance that what had happened to him all those years ago had little impact on the man he had become...the man he was this minute. The man holding Eva's hand, needing little else, yet burning for so very much more.

"I want to thank you for what you did back there," Eva said quietly, the pale moonlight illuminating her features.

"And here I thought you might object."

He felt rather than saw her gaze. "Why would you think that?"

He shrugged and tightened his grip on her hand. "Maybe what I said wasn't what you wanted me to tell your parents."

Maybe because I hadn't acted like the nerd you said you wanted me to be. A role he didn't want to play. Not now. Not tonight.

He heard her laugh, a soft sound that vied with the chirp of cicadas, and the hushed trembling of cyprus leaves in the light, humid breeze. "I have to say, I don't know what to make of your saying we were thinking about a church wedding." Apparently something occurred to her and she tried to remove her hand from his. He didn't allow her the escape.

"What?"

"I just realized that I should have told them long ago that Bill and I were considering a church wedding."

He tried to penetrate the darkness to see her eyes. "And had you?"

"What? Considered a church wedding? No. Bill refused to even talk about it." She brushed her free hand through her hair, then rested it against her neck. A place Adam would have liked to put his mouth. "I suggested we get married down here. But Bill, well, he wasn't interested in a full-blown family get-together." It was her turn to shrug and she dropped her hand from her neck. "That's how we ended up at the county courthouse."

She glanced at something unseen in the distance. Adam followed her gaze, hoping she hadn't spotted one of the agents. He had left a standing order that if he was anywhere in the vicinity, they were to move on to cover another area. He'd issued the request with the intention of keeping the entire property protected. Now he realized it also gave him a measure of privacy.

Eva sighed softly. "Anyway, what you said back there, the story you made up about how we met, it's better than reality. It almost makes me wish...."

Wish what, Eva? he silently demanded. *Say it.*

The silence stretched and he gently tugged on her hand to halt their steps. "Wish that it was the truth?" he murmured.

She tilted her chin toward the ground. "Yes."

She said the word so quietly it was almost lost in the untamed sounds of the bayou. But Adam heard it. And the sensations that expanded within him were coming to surpass what he felt for this woman sexually.

"Me, too," he murmured.

They stood like that for a long moment, their gazes locked, their clasped hands still. Adam swore he could hear the unsteady beat of his own heart.

Then Eva gave a quiet, nervous laugh and started walking again, pulling him gently along.

After a few feet, she looked in his direction. "What

you said about your family. That was the truth, wasn't it?"

"Yes."

They walked in silence until they reached the path in the trees. Adam reached out and parted the branches for her and Eva ducked inside.

"Do you regret it?" he asked.

She turned to wait as he slipped onto the path. "Regret what?"

"Your divorce."

She was quiet for a moment as she led them in the direction of the bayou. "No. I don't regret the marriage, either. They're both things I needed at the time."

The thick growth of trees lent a lush, almost cool quality to the air. "And the baby? Do you regret—"

"Never," she whispered.

A warm, bottomless admiration opened up in Adam for the remarkable woman next to him. That she should suffer through all she had and yet still have enough love—more love than anyone could touch—for the child growing within her, amazed him.

"What about now, Eva? What do you need now?"

She slowed again, then stopped altogether. Adam found himself wishing for at least the silvery light of the moon so he might see her.

"Now? Now I need much more."

More. That one word summed up precisely what Adam was coming to feel with each moment he spent near her. He was growing to want more. More out of the life he had forsaken for his career. More of the feelings he was just coming to know burgeoning inside him. Feelings Eva had shown him. Feelings he wanted to explore, both thrilled and awed that there might be no end to them.

Eva seemed to radiate a decisive energy as she gestured with her other hand. "I want to bridge this gap, this *canyon,* that's always existed between my father and me. I want a satisfying career with stress I can deal with. I want a..." She hesitated slightly, peering up at him. "I want a man who can be my partner, my best friend in every aspect of life, as well as in bed. I, um, want...no, I demand that he stick around for the bad times as well as the good. Not turn tail and run at the first sign of trouble." She stilled her hand on her lower stomach and stared at him, suddenly quiet. "And I want him to love this baby I'm going to have. I want him to be there for our child. And always be there for me, too."

Adam slid his gaze over her face, finding her more beautiful than any woman he'd ever known. "Basically, you want—"

"Everything," she murmured.

Everything.

Adam was just about to crush her to him and taste deeply of that mouth that offered strength and conviction as well as carnal pleasures, when she tugged on his hand.

"Come on. I want to show you my moon."

Her moon. A smile lit up his heart as she led him the remainder of the way down the path. He wanted to make fiery love to her in the golden light of "her moon." He wanted her cries of need to mingle with the sounds around them. To have her offer herself to him completely. To take as much as she gave. Then maybe he would feel more a part of this foreign, passionate, unique world she was raised in. They moved past the hulking warehouse, then stood on the dock, where the gentle waters of the river rippled against the shore.

Eva tried to lead him to the end of the dock, when he tugged on her hand. "No. Let's board the boat."

She stood there for a long moment, tension stiffening her shoulders.

"You've never been on it, have you?"

"No." Once again illuminated by the moon, he saw her look toward the bayou that branched off the river a mere few yards away. "But it doesn't matter."

"Yes, Eva, I can see it does," he murmured. "Let's board."

Without waiting for her response, he ushered her in the direction of the narrow plank that bridged the gap between the dock and the boat. Anchoring his hands against her oh-so-lush hips, he helped her across it, then jumped down after her onto the deck.

After unloading the cargo of oysters earlier in the day, Adam had helped Tolly scrub down the white-painted wood. While the faint odor of shellfish remained, so too did the scent of oil soap and a subtle fragrance of magnolias.

Eva freed herself from his grasp and crossed her arms tightly around her upper body.

"Have you ever told your father you'd like to go out on the boat with him?"

Eva slowly turned to face him. "What?"

He remained silent, watching her.

"Yes. I did once. When I was about ten. He told me this was men's work and I was to go play with my dolls or something."

"Sounds like Tolly." Adam chuckled softly. "And it sounds exactly like you."

"What sounds like me?"

"Oh, the fact that you only asked once."

She moved toward the stern of the boat and sat down on the padded seat, her knees tight, her hands loosely clasped in front of her. "I think you're coming to know far more about me than I'm comfortable with."

Adam took the seat next to her. "What would make you more comfortable?"

She didn't answer right away. He stretched his arm along the side of the boat, running his fingers over and down her bare shoulder. He reveled in the shiver that followed in its wake.

"It might help if you told me more about yourself," she said quietly.

He stilled his hand against her hot skin, feeling her intent gaze on him. It would be all too easy to give her the pat, easy answers he offered everyone else. But he sensed that, at this moment, he'd tell Eva anything she wanted to know. "Yes. Maybe it would." He tensed slightly. "What do you want me to tell you?"

She leaned back, snuggling into the crook of his arm. Instinctively, he curled that arm more tightly around her. "Oh, no. What you tell me I want you to offer."

That was a new one. Rubbing his chin against the top of her silky, fragrant hair, Adam thought about what he could tell her. Which was just about anything. Except his true reasons for being here.

She rested her hand against his thigh and the tension he felt shifted.

"Oh, I don't know. I suppose I could tell you that you drive me crazy when you touch me."

She squeezed his leg. "That's not what I meant."

He glanced down at her. "I know."

He settled more comfortably against the back of the boat. "Well, I suppose I could start by telling you I looked for my mother once."

Eva searched his face. "Did you find her?"

He nodded. Adam was amazed that he had not only said that, but that he was anxious for her response, her understanding. "I found her six years ago in a small town in Arizona, thirty miles or so southwest of Fort Defiance. She was living in a battered trailer, working at a truck stop."

Eva didn't say anything, but he could tell by her posture she was listening intently.

"She seemed to recognize me immediately. Surprising since she hadn't seen me in thirty years. But when I explained who I was, it was obvious I wasn't who she thought I was. This…this look of pain crossed her face, making her look twenty years older."

"Did she tell you why she gave you up?" Eva whispered.

At the memory, Adam grew rigid. "Yes. She took me inside, and over a cup of coffee she explained that she'd had to. That keeping me hurt too much."

"That doesn't make any sense."

"It didn't make much sense to me at the time either." He skimmed his thumb down the back of her arm, then slipped his hand under it, flattening his hand against her rib cage. "I guess it does now, though. Some. My father was a drifter of sorts. He left her almost as soon as he hooked up with her. She hadn't even known she was pregnant when he'd walked out. What she did know was that once I was born, I looked more like him than she could ever accept." He gazed out at the bayou. "I guess that explained the expression on her face when she first saw me."

He took a deep breath of the thick air. "I send her cards, you know, on Christmas and Mother's Day. One year I sent her a piece I found in a New York antique shop because it reminded me of her. She never writes back, though. But I'm okay with that."

There was a long silence. But not an uncomfortable one. Adam concentrated on the slow cadence of Eva's heartbeat under his hand. She made lazy circles on his leg with her index finger that stirred more than his libido.

"Did you ever think about looking for your father?"

"No."

Eva rubbed her cheek against his chest. Adam lifted his other hand to hold her there, scraping a thumb against her cheek.

"Who raised you?" she murmured. "Were you adopted?"

"I was raised in foster homes." He watched a mosquito land on his arm and pretended an interest in swatting at it.

Eva laughed quietly and scolded him for scratching.

He was raised in foster homes. That's the part that still bothered Adam. The ceaseless moving from home to home because his mother had held on to her parental rights to him until he was five, and by then he was unattractive adoption material. He'd been in good homes, and he'd been in bad. But what remained with him even now was the memory of countless other foster kids he'd been placed with over the years. The sounds of their quiet sobs in the dark of night when they thought no one was listening. Or perhaps they cried because they feared no one was listening. And often they were right. The majority of the foster parents, no matter how hard they tried, were emotionally unequipped to cater to a child whose heart was years in the breaking.

So at ten, Adam had reinforced his own lonely heart with imagined steel and convinced himself that family didn't exist in the form everyone dreamed about. And the cold statistics bore out his beliefs. A fifty percent divorce rate. A staggering number of children being raised by single parents. That's when he decided to devote his time to something that would permeate every aspect of his life, leaving little for him to give. Little for him to risk.

Sure, when he was thirteen, social services placed him in a home he stayed in for the remainder of his teenage years. But no matter how exceptional his final foster parents, Dan and Carol Richmond were, and how devoted they were to him and the other eight children they had taken in, it had been too late for Adam. He'd already made his decision about life. *His* life. And after a couple of semesters at college on scholarship, he found the FBI, and made the bureau and his career his family.

Eva gave a soft sigh. "I wonder if my son or daughter is going to want to know about Bill. And what I'm going to say when the time comes."

"The truth is always good," he murmured.

"Normally, yes." She paused for a long moment. "Tell me, Adam, what would you do if you found out your father left because he didn't want you?"

Adam remembered the divorce papers he had looked through earlier. And once again he was overcome by that same piercing anger he'd felt when he realized her ex had signed away his rights to their unborn baby. He didn't know what to say now. How to explain to Eva what he felt. Or how he might convince her that somehow her baby would be happy with the tremendous love she felt for it and the love her family would feel as well.

"I can tell you something else about myself that you might find surprising," he said, dreading that she might lead the conversation back to his upbringing if he didn't take command of the conversation.

"What?" she whispered, disappointment that he hadn't responded to her earlier question obvious in her response.

"That I envy you."

She tried to draw away as he knew she would, but he held her in place. "You envy me?"

"Uh-huh." He smoothed her hair away from her face. "I envy you your family. I envy you your roots. I even envy you your casual way of taking it all for granted."

He kissed the top of her sweet-smelling head. "I envy the way you and your father butt heads. Too stubborn to see how much you love each other. Too proud to admit that you're very much alike."

He stroked her lips with his thumb, holding her silenced.

"I envy that in a few months you're going to add to this family. And no matter how bad things look to you now, in the future you'll forget about this time. Forget how much you worried. And you'll only see the wonderful things created in this difficult time."

He hooked a finger under her chin and lifted her face to his. "I envy that you let a man into your heart, and hate that he hurt you because of your generous nature."

He held her gaze, the silvery moonlight reflecting off an unnatural shine to her eyes. "I envy you...you, Eva," he whispered roughly.

He lay his glasses on the seat, then brought his mouth down on hers. Silently telling her with the caress of his tongue that what he'd said was true. And her equivalent response told him she accepted and even hungrily welcomed it.

He skimmed her warm skin to rest his palm against her throat. Her low whimper told him she had some things of her own to say. Things he so longed to hear. But the time for words had passed. And now, it was time to let the conflicting emotions building within them take full life.

Unlike the flurried, hurried fumbling the night before, this kiss went deeper than mere physical need, an unexplainable attraction that could easily rage out of control. Just as Adam's need for her was growing to include so much more than her body.

The boat rocked gently and he drank in the subtle taste of salt from the gulf on her lips. He hauled her onto his lap. He guessed one could argue they didn't know each other well enough to consider taking their relationship to the intimate level he knew they would. Especially since the special woman in his arms was pregnant. And especially when he wasn't even sure he knew *himself* that well anymore.

He cradled her head in his hands, deepening the kiss, reveling in the feeling of her arms encircling him, her fingers entwining in the hair at the back of his neck. All he knew was that he liked the person he was when he was around Eva. Liked how she made him feel. Liked the way she made him take another, fresh look at the world. Making him believe, for the first time, that emotions weren't fickle, fleeting passions that would burn out as quickly as they fired up, with little regard for the pain they left behind. Because though he might have been wrong on a lot of points since initially accepting this assignment, he was sure of one thing: Eva would be the one woman he would never forget. His time with her would not be a fling to be filed along with the others. She had reached in and touched something elemental within him so effortlessly, so unknowingly, that he couldn't help feeling she was special.

Eva slid one leg to the deck of the boat, never breaking their kiss as she straddled him.

This time, she didn't need to coax him to touch her breasts. He did so on his own. Dropping his hands to her silky, slick shoulders, he slowly pushed the thin straps of her dress aside, revealing her glistening skin in the moonlight. Her dress fell away and bunched around her waist like a whisper. Her breasts strained against the strapless bra she wore, nearly spilling out of the top. She dropped her head back, letting him take his fill as he slid his hands under the fullness of her breasts, rasping the pads of his thumbs across the nipples that made dark circles under the thin white lace of her bra. With a groan, he dipped his thumbs under the material, urging both peaks out. He caught the rigid tip of the right one between his thumb and index finger, then lowered his mouth to capture the other, thinking nothing had ever tasted sweeter.

Eva shuddered and scooted closer so the only things separating them were his slacks and her panties. Suckling more deeply, he slid his other hand down the length of her slender waist, past her dress, to her thigh, following the soft flesh inward until the tip of his index finger rested on the elastic of her panties. Eva rotated her hips, the movement nearly forcing his finger inside her underwear, encouraging the contact he sought. Then she tensed. He stopped his ascent, then realized she hadn't frozen in fear, but in anticipation.

He slid his finger inside, finding her slick and hot. A low groan escaped her mouth and she grabbed at his shirt, undoing the buttons, tugging the material aside and pressing her palms against his chest. Adam abandoned his laving of her breasts and pulled her flush against him, reveling in the brush of her satiny softness against his hair-covered skin. He brought his mouth down on hers with hot intent, lost in her response.

Lord, how he was coming to want this woman. Every part of her. He yearned to possess her mind, body and soul. He longed to brand her with his passion, as she was branding him. Most of all, he wanted her to know that she meant so much more to him than just rapid breathing and searching hands. He wanted to tell her in every way he knew how that she was special. That the way she made him feel was special. That what they were experiencing, no matter how fleeting, was special.

Holding her head against his with one hand, he pushed the crotch of her panties aside with the other. He found her silky nub and drew tiny circles around and around before pressing intently, urgently, against it. He swallowed her soft cry, thrusting his tongue deep into her mouth, welcoming the answering thrust of hers. He slipped the tip of his index finger into her wetness even as he kept up the slow circling of his thumb, finding her tight, sleek, needy. He dipped his finger in a little more deeply then withdrew, finding a natural rhythm that would heighten her passion, but not draw her too near the edge. No. He wanted to be with her, feel with her, share with her the wondrous moment when she came apart.

She dragged her mouth slightly away from his. "Please," she said, her fingers moving wildly through his hair, pulling him away, drawing him near.

He withdrew his finger, put together two, then thrust them in deeply at once, readying her for him, trying to make the moment when he entered her pleasurable.

She thrust her hips forward, against his hand, wanting more, increasing his need to give her what she craved. But not yet. He didn't want to end it yet. He wanted to savor these incredible sensations with Eva. Draw them out, build them up, then finally, urge them to climb to their ultimate climax.

She fumbled with the button of his slacks, and within moments her slender hand grazed the length of his erection. She pulled him out and her fingers wrapped around his width. Then she slid her hand slowly up and down, up and down, matching the rhythm of his fingers inside her, driving him wild, out of his mind with need.

She worked her way to his ear, laving the outer shell, then searing a path down his neck and back up to his mouth. Adam was filled with the need to be inside her, to feel her slick muscles around him, to watch her mirror the movements of her hand with her body. Then he realized the one thing that would make the fantasy reality was missing. He didn't have a condom.

The revelation came on the brink of climax. Thrusting his fingers more deeply inside her, his thumb working madly, he didn't allow himself the release until he heard her sharp intake of breath, her echoing cry...then he followed right after her, reveling in the tightness of her hand around him even as he bucked against it, keeping up the rhythm of his fingers, even as she melted around him. The sultry heat of the night moved in him and around him. Fusing him with the woman on his lap. Joining their harsh breaths as they sought air. Intensifying their kiss as she pressed her open mouth against his.

For several long moments they stayed like that, rocking with the aftershocks, and clinging to each other like the Spanish moss that covered the nearby live oaks. Feeling the contractions of her muscles ease, he slowly slipped his fingers out and grasped either side of her head, ending their kiss.

"More," she murmured ardently, her eyes dark with passion, her body even now seeking him, rubbing against the length of him.

"No, Eva. No more. Not now."

Maybe not ever. He closed his eyes and languidly claimed her lips one last time. God, if her mere touch could do so much to him, he couldn't fathom what might happen if they made love.

He pulled her away again and slowly began straightening her dress. "We have to go back now, Eva."

"Back...yes."

He captured her gaze, reading the passionate hope in her eyes. He shook his head. "I'm not going to sleep with you tonight."

She started to say something then caught her bottom

lip between her straight white teeth. She blinked back what he guessed might be tears of frustration. It struck him with fierce intensity that she might think he didn't want her because she was pregnant. Pregnant with another man's child. Even though that couldn't be further from the truth—or maybe nearer than he thought— Adam wouldn't allow himself to soothe her pain. He couldn't. No matter how much he wanted to make love to Eva, he couldn't allow himself the ultimate mind-blowing pleasure. Could never claim her as completely as he was coming to want to. Because what lay at the bottom was his knowledge that Eva was not his for the taking. And she never would be. Not because of his assignment. Not even because she was unwilling to give herself to him. But because he would never, could never, let her.

Deep down in the dark shadows of his soul, Adam knew he could never be the *everything* Eva Mavros Burgess wanted. The everything she—and her child—deserved.

9

EVA WAS TORN. Between life as she knew it...and the reality that Adam had a large part in changing.

Reality.

Sitting on the wooden seat of the swing that hung from the old willow tree in the front yard, the early-morning sun dappling the grass around her feet, Eva questioned the meaning of the word. Especially within the framework of her present situation. She tightened her hands on the swing's ropes, wondering where Adam had slept last night. Wondering further why it hurt so that he had refused her, rejected her in the light of her moon.

She had awakened a half hour earlier, hot and bothered, and very alone. She had taken a cool shower, but the water did little to alleviate the sultry heat pressing in and around her. Rather than going to the kitchen where her mother and grandmother were, she'd slipped out the front door and sat in the swing. Above her, warblers and mourning doves called to each other.

If anyone had told her the week before that she had the capacity to love again, Eva would have shot the messenger for being insane. She smoothed her hands over her slightly rounded stomach, then rested them there, reminding herself of the reason she hadn't intended to date another man, much less find herself falling in love with one. At least until the child she carried had graduated from college sometime far into the future.

Then again, if somebody had told her three months ago that she would be divorced and pregnant, she would have shot that person as well.

She rested her cheek against one of the ropes and tried to make sense out of the emotions ebbing and flowing through her.

Bill. Nothing. Closing her eyes and breathing in the heady scent of jasmine, she tried to summon some sort of remorse for having little feeling for her ex-husband. As it was, she was finding it difficult to imagine what he looked like. Not the specifics. Those, of course, she saw clearly. But she couldn't seem to isolate the individual expressions that defined their relationship. She was having a harder time, still, reinforcing any of her own distant emotions for him, except for the dull pain she felt at his betrayal.

Had their relationship been so shallow that she could forget him so easily? Or was her growing affection for Adam—and the lack of feeling for Bill—not to be trusted? If Adam had allowed their so very tentative relationship to advance the way she had wanted the night before, would she have awakened this morning filled with regret? Or would that have come somewhere down the road when the newness faded?

An ache the size of Louisiana filled her chest. At that moment, she couldn't imagine any of the many wonderful sensations she felt for Adam fading. When he touched her, something elemental responded, something so elusive, she suspected it flowed from a source greater than her.

But the very fact that the explanation was elusive made her warier of that source. How could she fall for another man when just a few scant weeks ago, she'd thought herself in love with Bill?

No, that wasn't true. She had never really been "in" love with Bill. She knew that the minute she'd accepted his cool marriage proposal a year before. Instead her reaction had been similar to the feeling she experienced when adding up long columns of debits and credits, and finding they reconciled. It had nothing to do with love, but rather a calm acceptance that she would never find that one person who would sweep her off her feet.

Then there was Adam.

Idly pushing a foot against the soft earth, Eva brought the swing to a lazy rock. Her body tingled and a liquid yearning pooled in her belly at the mere thought of Adam and what he had done to her the night before. Her feelings for him, and his apparent attraction for her, refused to be neatly tucked into columns of any sort.

And it was the very nature of those feelings that caused her to doubt them.

Pushing herself off the swing, Eva smoothed her dress, then stepped toward the house that shone almost pink in the hazy morning sun. She longed to turn to her mother for advice, but that was out of the question, given her little ruse.

She swept through the house and entered the kitchen where she listlessly greeted her mother and grandmother where they sat in their usual chairs. She made herself a cup of herb tea, then sat down at the table.

"Did Papa and Adam go oystering again?" Her question was more of a comment, an acceptance that of course her father would take Adam oystering with him, than a need for an answer.

Her grandmother eyed her over the rim of her reading glasses. "Yes, they did. They said they'd be back early this morning."

Eva blew on the steaming surface of her tea, then took a sip, gazing at the one-foot-long, two-feet-wide blanket draped across her grandmother's lap. A blanket that grew stitch by wondrous stitch as she worked. Eva reached out and lovingly fingered the soft, colorful creation.

"It's pretty," she murmured, running her fingertips over the perfect loops.

Her mother's chair creaked as she shifted, working on what looked like a tiny sweater. "I think the baby will like it. It's heavy enough for winter in New Jersey."

Winter. As in next March. Her due date.

Eva smiled. She hadn't officially told her mother or grandmother about the baby yet. But somehow both of them knew.

In the weeks since she'd found out she was pregnant, Eva had had a hard time accepting it in the midst of everything else that had happened. Now she reveled in the surge of warmth and expectation that spread across her chest.

Tears pricked the corner of her eyes and she moved her hand back to hold her teacup. She was *not* going to cry.

"You and Adam must be very excited," her mother said.

She and Adam? Added on top of the contradictory emotions already vying for attention in her heart, Eva didn't feel up to dealing with how much she *would* like it if Adam was excited about the baby. Or the feeling that she would give everything that was her, everything Adam said he envied, if only the child was his.

A fat, hot tear rolled down her cheek and she rubbed it away. The harsh truth was that this child wasn't Adam's. He wasn't even her husband.

And the fact that the two precious women next to her knew nothing about that truth suddenly overwhelmed her.

Unable to blink them back, tears popped over her lower lashes. Eva tightened her fingers around her cup.

"Oh, Mama, what have I done?"

ADAM READJUSTED the dredge lever, the hazy sun hot on his shoulders, the thick, salty smell of the gulf filling his nose.

"Bring it up that way," Tolly shouted from the other side of the boat.

Adam did, then released the lever, his present chore done.

Sitting in the seat where he and Eva had nearly made love the night before, he reached for the thermos of coffee Tolly gave him earlier. He poured out the last of the still-warm liquid.

"My daughter, she locked you out of the bedroom last night, no?" Tolly overturned a bucket then sat in front of Adam.

Adam took his time sipping the coffee from the plastic cup, weighing his response. He couldn't very well deny that he and Eva had slept apart. Tolly had shaken him awake at four that morning where he lay on the front-porch swing, hours after he'd forced Eva to go upstairs…alone.

"Actually, no. It was too hot and I couldn't sleep so I went for a walk. Falling asleep on the swing was an accident."

Adam dragged the back of his hand across his damp forehead, hating to continue this charade. Playing roles was part of his job, and he'd never had a problem keeping in character…until now. Lying to Eva's family was becoming harder and harder.

Tolly hmmphed and Adam eyed him warily. Lying to Tolly was especially difficult because Adam had the distinct feeling the weathered Greek didn't believe a word he said. Briefly, he was thankful Tolly Mavros was an honest man, because he would be deadly if he were a criminal.

"An accident," Tolly repeated, pushing the bill of his fisherman's cap back on his head.

"Certainly, over the years you and Katina have slept apart every now and again."

"Never." Tolly passionately waved his meaty hand. "Not one night in almost thirty-five years of marriage."

Adam raised an eyebrow, believing him. "Not once?"

Tolly gave his graying bushy eyebrows a quick raise and brought his head up once with a terse *tsk* that Adam had come to see was his way of answering in the negative.

He grinned. "You have a good marriage, then."

"The best," Tolly gruffly agreed. "But it is not my marriage I'm worried about."

Adam stared down into his empty cup, giving vent to a series of silent curses. He'd stepped right into that one.

For what seemed to be the millionth time, he vehemently questioned Eva's motives for setting up this scheme. While he recognized that even she couldn't have known things would spin so out of control, how could she continue with a plan that had lost its viability after the first night?

He watched Tolly take his cap off. He rubbed the wrist of his long-sleeved shirt across his forehead then plunked the fisherman's cap back down on top of his salt-and-pepper hair. Adam could certainly sympathize with Eva's motives. Tolly was a rough man who lived by traditional rules that were hard and fast. And the breaking of those rules likely exacted a response few people could live with. The past two mornings had made Adam wish he'd had a father who cared about his family the way Tolly obviously cared about his own. But he wasn't foolish enough to believe that living with his overbearing ways would have been easy. He could even see how feelings of animosity and detachment could develop, being under the constant thumb of the well-meaning but brusque man. But didn't Eva understand that she was only making matters worse?

Damn, but he had gotten himself into a mess with this case. Forget that he'd mucked things up terribly by losing focus on the case itself, rendering him completely unprepared for the break-in yesterday. He couldn't fight the feeling that he'd gotten himself in way over his head personally as well as professionally. And *that* was what scared him more than anything else.

"Do you love my Eva?" Tolly asked abruptly.

Shocked out of his uncomfortable reverie, Adam shifted his gaze to the older man's face.

"Love her?" Remembering his role, he pushed up his glasses. "Of course I love her. I wouldn't have married her otherwise."

Tolly stared at him unblinkingly.

Adam shifted. He was going to have to do better than that. "I love her insofar as my definition of love goes," he said. "She...satisfies something inside of me."

Tolly made a fist out of one hand and tapped it against his own head. "Here?" He moved the fist to his chest. "Here?" Then he dropped it to his groin. "Or here?"

Adam could have said all three and suspected he was coming to mean it. Which was a revelation in itself. Instead he fisted his own right hand. "Sure, I feel it in those places. But mostly I feel it here." He nestled his fist against his solar plexus, thinking the imagery of the fist accurately portrayed the knotted emotions lodged directly in the area he indicated. Emotions he didn't have to pretend. Feelings that were there whether he wanted them to be or not. Tight sensations he feared he'd never rid himself of…not with one passionate, steamy night with Eva, or a thousand.

Tolly's grin was brighter than any Adam had seen him give. He reached out and slapped Adam's shoulder. "Good."

Tolly got up and began whistling as he returned to work. Adam couldn't help thinking he'd just been outsmarted by a man who was wiser than he had given him credit for.

Grinning wryly, he surmised he hadn't been the only one outwitted. Eva had been, too. Because Tolly Mavros's questioning told Adam that he must have seen those divorce papers on the floor of Eva's bedroom yesterday. Tolly's behavior also told him that despite his traditional values, it didn't much matter to him. Not so long as everything would be right from there on out.

Adam swiped at a dragonfly as it zoomed past his ear in the humid air. Making everything right was a promise he couldn't make. Not to Tolly. Not to Eva either.

"Funny you should mention love, Tolly," he said quietly. "Because I get the impression that your daughter questions your love for her."

Tolly's whistling stopped abruptly, but he continued working, his back to Adam. He mumbled something in Greek. "Nonsense. My daughter questions no such thing."

Adam got up from the bench, grabbing on to a rope hanging from the dredger and lazily leaning his weight against it. "No?"

"No." Tolly's movements were jerky and impatient.

"She thinks everything she does makes you unhappy."

"Nonsense," he said again.

Adam squinted in the hazy sunlight. "You know, it might be a good idea to let her know your feelings every now and again."

"She knows my feelings." He gestured around the deck. "I named my boat for her, no?"

"A boat she's never been on," Adam said, neglecting to mention their interlude last night. He drew a long breath. "You've never told her you love her, have you?"

Tolly finally stopped working and stared at him. Long moments slid by with nothing but the sound of buzzing flies, the lap of the water against the boat and the call of a bird nearby. "Love, you show. Not tell."

Adam gave the old salt a sad smile. "Then maybe you should brush up on your showing, Tolly. Because there's been a breakdown in communications and Eva's getting the wrong messages."

Tolly made his usual hmmph and Adam pushed away from the rope. But as he bent to pick up the coffee thermos, he saw Tolly staring out thoughtfully across one of his privately owned beds. Maybe, just maybe, he had reached the crusty Greek. The way Adam figured it, if he couldn't make things right between himself and Eva, at least he could try to repair the ties between father and daughter. Ties he had never had with either of his parents. Ties he now saw were more precious than gold.

He twisted the cap back onto the thermos. If everything was all right between Eva and Tolly, it would make his own leaving that much easier. But was it easier for them...or himself?

EVA HAD TRIED to get Adam alone to explain what happened that morning. But between her mother's insistence that she needed help with dinner, and her grandmother's trying to teach her how to crochet, Eva hadn't a moment to herself. She stood in the kitchen doorway, trying to get Adam's attention where he sat at the dining-room table. But her father was talking to him in hushed tones so that all Eva could do was drop her hand back to her side and give herself over to the inevitable fact that Adam would have to deal with this one on his own.

"Here, take this in," her mother said, pushing a platter of grilled pork chops into her hands.

Eva stared at the meat, waiting for her stomach to churn, relieved when nothing but a growl materialized. Thank God. Her doctor had told her that her second trimester would be much easier than her first. She swallowed. She'd also told her that her sex drive would return tenfold. Eva eyed Adam and the way his shower-damp hair curled over his shirt collar, thinking that on both counts, she couldn't find cause for argument.

Stepping into the dining room, she placed the platter the middle of the table. Adam's gaze lingered on the many buttons up the front of her dress, then he looked up to her. She nodded her head in the direction of the living room, attempting to communicate that she needed to talk to him. Tolly slapped his hand on his arm to regain Adam's attention.

Eva wilted under the pressure as she glanced toward her father. *Oh, God, what had she done?*

Within minutes everyone was settled around the table and, as Eva feared, her mother clanked her fork against her wineglass.

"Everyone, I have an announcement to make," Katina said.

Eva cringed. Seeing as everyone but her father and

brother already knew the news, this was hardly *Herald* material. She fastened a smile onto her face.

"Adam and Eva are expecting their first child."

"Hear, hear," her grandmother said next to her.

Across the table her brother, Pete, looked briefly as if he'd lost his best friend, then sat back in his chair, a surprised smile on his handsome face.

And Tolly was heartily slapping Adam on the back as if he'd just shot some prized deer.

But all of that disappeared as Adam's shocked gaze met with Eva's across the table.

I'm sorry, she tried to convey.

Why didn't you tell me they knew, his expression answered.

Then something unexpected happened. A light so affectionate, so wonderful, warmed the depths of Adam's eyes. Eva's heart did a funny little turn, a surreal cloud rushing to envelope her so that for one precious moment, she believed she was married to Adam. That the baby she carried was theirs. Her chest filled with hope, her cheeks flushed in shared intimacy, her body called out its need for the man across from her.

Her father's rough but gentle hand on her arm tugged her attention to his familiar, craggy face. "You have brought this family much happiness, Eva."

As rapidly as it gathered, the cloud vanished. Eva stared at the harsh truth even as she looked into her father's proud face. *It's all a lie, Papa*, she wanted to say. *All of it. Adam's not my husband. The child I carry was fathered by a man you don't even know. And you never will because he wants nothing to do with the baby.* She felt lightheaded and leaned her head against her hand, wondering if she would go from morning sickness to fainting dead away.

"Eva, are you all right?" She heard Adam's voice

above all others as her father moved his hand to her back to steady her.

Taking the glass of water her grandmother offered, Eva lifted it to her lips. She took a long sip, then drew the cool glass across her hot forehead. The dizziness passed and she managed a small, shaky smile to everyone but her father. Him, she couldn't face. She might never be able to face him again.

"I'm fine. It must be the heat."

"And the excitement," her mother added.

How Eva managed to get through the remainder of the long meal she didn't know. Talk was full of childhood milestones, Eva's own misdeeds, and of course all the things that needed to be done before welcoming the latest addition to the family.

In a small way, Eva was glad that some of her news was out. Sure, the priorities had switched—she had planned to tell them about her divorce first, then the baby. But she hadn't reckoned on her mother and grandmother's uncanny perception. And she certainly hadn't foreseen the wild turn her once-safe relationship with Adam would take.

Finally, everybody had eaten their fill. Her father and grandmother went upstairs for their naps, her brother left the house, and Eva and Adam helped clear the table, the unspoken tension between them nearly visible. Her mother shooed her out of the kitchen and told her to take a siesta with Adam. Eva turned around to see that he had overheard the command, an unspoken question in his eyes. Eva flushed, telling herself he was being ridiculous. Despite the heat that had flared between them the night before, ultimately he had pushed her away.

Then why did he look as if he'd like nothing better than to peel her dress away from her hot skin and spend the rest of the afternoon making up for lost time? And why did she want him to do that more than anything?

"Uh, I think I'd rather go for a walk," Eva said quietly, tearing her gaze from Adam's. "You know, to burn off some of those calories I put away."

"I'll go with you," Adam said.

Eva held the screen door for him as he stepped out. Then she carefully closed the door so it didn't give it usual slap against the frame. She crossed her arms over her chest and led the way across the grass. Only in passing did she realize this was the same path they'd taken the night before. But this time, her moon was no where to be seen. And hopefully she wouldn't make the same mistakes she'd made last night.

"You told them," Adam said quietly, his presence powerful one next to her.

Eva nodded. "I thought maybe it would be best after what, you know, you said on the boat last night."

She looked at him to find his gaze heady and curious.

"You know, about this baby not just belonging to me, but to them too. You were right."

He was silent for a long moment. The thick air magnified the vivid colors of the Spanish moss and magnolias, lending a magical quality to the day. Above them, clouds writhed and wrinkled and swirled continually, driven by the gentle gulf breezes. The atmosphere of calm was like that of Eden where time seemed to stop. But the calm was as deceptive as the serenity Eva tried to affect. At any moment, a wild storm could break loose. Just like the storm swirling in her.

"I don't suppose I have to ask if you told them about me."

"No," she said, averting her gaze. "I couldn't do that. Not…not yet."

His strong grip on her shoulders startled her into stopping. He pulled her to face him.

"Eva, there's nothing I'd like more than to be the father of that child you're carrying. To claim him or her as mine. You as mine. But the facts are that neither of you *are* mine. You deserve to know that, too. I deserve that."

Eva's gaze roamed from his dark gold eyebrows, down to the delectable dimple in his chin, finding a pained honesty on his face that twisted her gut. She hesitantly reached out to touch his cheek, but he pulled away.

"Damn it, somewhere over these past couple of days, the line between what's real and what's not has disappeared. I don't know when, I don't know how, but I've even begun to wonder what it would be like if I *was* your husband. Imagining what the future would hold for us as a couple. Picturing what it would be like to be a father, a part of this family…a part of our family." He took her hand. "I see myself waking up with you every morning, Eva, and it causes something I don't know how to describe to grow in my chest. Something wonderful, magical, passionate. I dream of burying myself between your legs for long hours on end, making all your secret fantasies come true… indulging in my own."

He released her, restlessly paced away, then stalked back to her. "You know the fantasy I had when I first spotted you at the firm? In my mind, I saw you wearing nothing but a little bikini, stretched out on the deck of a boat I have moored in Delaware Bay, your skin glistening in the sun. A boat I bought three years ago and have never even taken out because buying it seemed like a good idea at the time, but it's not important enough for me to make time for. And my image of you lying across the deck in that bikini was nothing but a stupid, adolescent fantasy."

Eva flinched. "Adam, I—"

"Facts are facts, and the fact we have to face here is that there's no 'our' anywhere in this equation. I'm playing a role for you, nothing more, nothing less. No matter how much I wish differently. There's no going back now, Eva. We've charted this damn course for ourselves, and we're just going to have to play it out on the calmest waters possible."

As abruptly as his tirade began, it ended. Eva didn't know what to say. So she didn't say anything. Instead she did something she'd been doing a lot lately in the past two days: acted on impulse. And the one now clamoring for attention was that she desperately needed to kiss Adam.

Clamping her hand around the back of his neck, she hauled his head down and roughly brought his mouth against hers. With wild, hungry, deep flicks of her tongue, she drank in the passion left by his words. Tasting the bittersweet remnants of wine. Telling him with her kiss that she felt as confused and needy and achy as he did...and telling him that right now, right this moment, it didn't matter. Nothing did. Not as long as they could share their hunger. Not as long as she could feel the heat of his body, leaving her wistful and feminine and yearning. Not as long as he felt the same way she did.

The sun on her hair was hot and penetrating as Eva stepped closer to him, welcoming his hands on her hips, gasping when he dragged her against his hard length, pressing his erection against the soft flesh of her stomach. Spontaneously, Eva rocked against him, relishing his almost inaudible groan.

The slap of the screen door some fifty yards away was like a gunshot. Eva broke away from the kiss, her heart pounding erratically in her chest, her blood flowing thickly through her veins. A furtive glance toward the house found no one in sight, leaving her to think someone had just gone in. And had likely stood witness to her and Adam's passionate display.

When she turned back around, she found Adam striding purposefully toward the path in the trees.

The urge to rush after him swept through her limbs. But instead she stood frozen, knowing deep down that he needed time to himself. Time to make sense out of what was happening to him, if there was any sense to be made.

She pressed her fingertips to her temples. *Could* it work out between them? Was she willing to let him into her life all the way? Was he even willing to give her, or the two of them as a couple, a chance? Or did he feel as overwhelmed as she did, not knowing which way to go, and unclearer still about the emotions that might lead to the most exquisite love either of them had ever shared, or the most ripping heartbreak?

By the time Eva made her way through the path and emerged from the trees, Adam was nowhere to be seen. She looked first to the boat, rocking slightly, but otherwise empty, then the open doors to the warehouse. Nothing.

Pushing damp tendrils of hair back and holding them at her nape, she slowly made her way toward the warehouse.

Once in the musty confines of the office, she pounded on her laptop keyboard, immersing herself in numbers and the way they neatly added up, reconciled. She divided them into separate spreadsheets, other accounting sheets, but still the result was the same: they added up. No emotions involved here, only a keen sense of ultimate simplicity. And she managed to do the work it normally would have taken her half a day to complete in one hour. But rather than the relief she usually felt, the sense of accomplishment, Eva felt drained, unsatisfied, unchallenged. The accounting was done. There were no other numbers to add. No other chores to perform. And the amounts that had so captured her attention transformed into nothing but sheets full of numbers, dull, lifeless and unattractive.

For one numbing second, Eva caught a glimpse of what the rest of her life might hold.

The clang of something metallic outside the office sounded. She glanced absently in the direction of the door window. Is that what her life had been? An emotionless void in which she functioned in no more an important manner than a machine? Afraid to explore other horizons? Scared she might find out she'd made a mistake so many years ago when she left Belle Rivage and the overbearing presence of her father? Trading it instead for a life without emotion, without love?

Getting up from the chair, she opened the office door. She could see nothing in the shadowy darkness of the warehouse. The sound must have come from outside. Moving toward the open doors—the wide portal made unusually bright by the hazy afternoon sunshine—she wondered if Adam had come to seek her out. The anticipation that coursed through her as she stepped outside only proved even more how empty her life had become.

Eva caught a glimpse of Adam near the boat, but he wasn't alone. She recognized the slightly bowed posture of her brother standing awkwardly next to Adam. Her heart gave a gentle squeeze. In all her planning, Eva hadn't taken a moment to consider the effect her return with Adam would have on Pete. That he might feel threatened by the presence of another man in their father's life. A man who could challenge him for his already tenuous position of being the next head of the household. Someone who could definitely rival him for the affections of their father, a man who gave his love so sparingly already.

Or maybe she was way off and that's not what had been bothering her brother. While she and Pete were close, she had always suspected there were some things he couldn't share with her. Was he sharing those thoughts with Adam now?

Eva leaned against the warm metal of the warehouse and watched the two men on the dock. They made a striking contrast against the backdrop of the bayou, both of them in their dinner clothes, Adam a tall, solid and yes, athletic figure, Pete slightly shorter, stockier, a younger version of Tolly. In the three days they'd been there, Eva couldn't recall Adam talking to her brother at all, aside from obligatory, friendly exchanges. But he did so now with a quiet urgency she could sense even from there. And when Adam put his hand on Pete's shoulder and pulled him to his side, Eva realized that he must be telling her brother he had nothing to fear from his presence. That his addition—no matter how temporary Eva knew it to be—wouldn't affect Pete's relationship with their father.

For the second time that day, Eva blinked back hot tears.

Another metallic sound echoed through the warehouse and she jumped. Had Jimmy been inside without her knowing? She turned back toward the doors, but could see little in the inky blackness. The slam of the door against the metal wall in the office clattered through the warehouse, then a figure raced past her, nearly knocking her down. Eva stood speechless as a man wearing a beige fishing hat and hunting vest cut a path through the gravel leading to the road, then disappeared into a thicket of trees…her laptop computer tucked under one arm.

"Adam." His name caught in her throat.

10

ADAM HAD SEEN the unfamiliar figure dash across the warehouse lot clutching Eva's laptop computer but had been too far away to have any hope of catching him. This time his image as a nerd had nothing to do with his decision. The gig was up. It was simple as that. If his mind had been working correctly, he would have realized the whole operation was compromised the day before with the ransacking of Eva's bedroom.

On the way back to the house, he'd spotted the two backup agents standing near the path and waved them off. Evidently they hadn't caught the thief either. And what Adam had to do now, he had to do alone. This went far deeper than the simple theft of Eva's laptop.

In the house, he ushered Eva up to her bedroom, where he carefully explained to her his true identity as a forensic accountant for the FBI's Financial Crimes Unit. And his motivations for accepting her bizarre request that he play the role of her husband. He wasn't sure what her reaction would be. A part of him hoped it would be anger at having been betrayed by another male...the same way her ex-husband had betrayed her. And when he wound his explanation down, purposely leaving out all the acute, personal revelations being with her had forced on him, he searched her impassive face. Trying to read her thoughts. Wanting her to hate him so it would make everything that happened from there on easier for them both.

"So ultimately I didn't agree to be your husband because you might give me a good recommendation on my next job review. Because I'm not going to be at Sheffert, Logan and Brace long enough to make that date. I'm here because I needed to see if you knew anything about Sheffert's dirty dealings. And to determine if you are involved." He dragged in a breath. "That's about the brunt of it," he said with deliberate harshness, striving to achieve the objectivity he so needed to see this case through to its conclusion.

Eva said nothing for a long minute. Instead, she just stood staring at him silently, maddeningly calm, and altogether too appealing.

"I know," was all she said.

Adam eyed her, wondering if she had heard a single word he'd said. Hadn't he just coldly told her she was nothing more than a means to an end in his investigation of Norman Sheffert? Hadn't he implied with his poker-faced expression that whatever had happened between them had occurred within the confines of his case, and therefore didn't matter?

Yes. So then why was she looking at him as if she wanted him, yearned for him, all the more?

"What?" he asked, the word coming out more of a murmur.

"I said I know." She finally tugged that poignant gaze from his and stepped over to the dresser. "At least about your not being who you pretended to be. After our first kiss, well, I suspected you couldn't be the man I thought I knew. At least not the geek I met. And after the night at the table when you…and on the boat afterward…" She glanced at him over her shoulder. "I didn't know you were an FBI field agent, but I knew you had to be something other than what you were pretending to be." Her voice dropped to a whisper. "There were too many pieces that didn't fit. Too many inconsistencies in your behavior…in your sharing of your background."

"But I betrayed you," he said, not quite believing that she could be so accepting, so understanding.

She slowly shook her head. "No, you didn't betray me, Adam. You were doing your job. You couldn't have known what would happen between us. I didn't know." She leaned against an iron bedpost and dropped her gaze. "What matters is that you told me the truth now, when it matters."

A profound relief enveloped Adam. He was hard-pressed not to haul her into his arms. Bury his nose in her sweet-smelling hair, crush her all-too-lush body to his. But he couldn't give himself over to such forgetfulness. He had a job to do. Something he had somehow forgotten over the past three days. Something he needed to concentrate on now. No matter how much he'd like to push all that aside and devote the next few hours to Eva and Eva alone.

"So," she said quietly. "What conclusion did you come to about me and my possible involvement with Sheffert?"

"That you're not. Involved, I mean." He took off his glasses, finally glad to be rid of them. Wishing he could rid himself of his need for the woman in front of him as easily.

She gazed at him long and hard. Then she gave him a soft, sexy smile. "All along I knew there was much more behind those glasses than an inexperienced nerd."

"It doesn't bother you? To find out I lied about my true identity? That for a time, anyway, I considered you a suspect?"

She caught her bottom lip between her teeth, then re-leased it.

She gazed down at where she worried her hands in

front of her. "Yes, it does. But there's more involved here than phantom ledgers and tax evasion, isn't there?"

He scanned her body from head to foot, hesitating at her waist. A waist that was still narrow and fit, but would soon be swollen with the child she carried. But his feelings for her went oh so much deeper than physical desire. Despite Eva Burgess's pregnancy, he wanted her, longed for her, needed her in a way that scared him to death.

Yes, there was far more at work here than his assignment.

"My gun."

Eva blinked and Adam knew that she didn't have any knowledge of its whereabouts.

"It came up missing after the break-in."

"I…I didn't know you had a gun."

Adam stepped nearer to her and gently grasped her arms. "Eva, now that I don't have to pussyfoot around, is there anything odd you've come across in the time you've worked for Sheffert? Any accounts that didn't make sense? Anything that struck you as unusual?"

She started to shake her head, apparently searching her memory, even as she swallowed hard. The skin of her arms was silky and hot under his fingers. He realized he'd abandoned his urgent grip and was now caressing her, drawing goose bumps he wanted to smooth.

"Wait," she said, her gaze fastening on his. A gaze jam-packed with conflicting emotions. "Yesterday when I tried to access one of the Honeycutt diskettes I took from Sheffert's office, I found some sort of game."

"A game?" Adam repeated, forcing himself to release her for fear that he wouldn't be able to stop touching her no matter how important the conversation.

"Yes." She shrugged and crossed her arms, giving a shiver. "I found it odd, but when I realized the disk didn't have what I needed on it, I put it aside."

"Do you have it?"

She went to her attaché case and slipped a black three-and-a-half-inch disk out of an inside pocket. "My brother has a PC in his room. You can check it out there."

Adam flipped the disk over in his fingers.

"Eva, I'm sorry."

She blinked at him several times, apparently trying to discern the meaning of his words.

Finally, she smiled in a way that was sad and provocative all at the same time. She tucked her hair behind her ear and lifted her chin. "Yes, so am I."

Adam wrenched his gaze from her alluring face and strode toward the door.

"What are we going to tell my family?" she asked, catching him before he walked out.

He took in the view of her standing next to that bed, wanting to tell her to say nothing. To let him have just one more day as their son-in-law. More important, he longed to ask her for one more night as her husband. To allow him to indulge himself just a little longer. Instead he said, "Tell them whatever you need to. But know this. Everyone here is safe. So you don't have anything to worry about there."

Somewhere deep down, he knew he was putting the ball in her court. The case might be over, but that didn't mean they had to be, did it?

EVA DIDN'T TELL *her parents.*

That awareness crowded everything else from Adam's head as he slipped the Honeycutt diskette into Pete's PC, then slid a glance at the woman in the chair next to him.

Over the course of the past hour, he'd locked himself up in Tolly's warehouse office making calls. Weckworth had been less than overjoyed to hear from him.

"Where in the hell have you been, Grayson? Damn it, I was expecting you to call me back after you reported that break-in yesterday."

Adam had reminded Weckworth that he wasn't in the midst of the Aryans in Search of Domination group where his life had been in danger every moment of every day. But being filled in on the theft of Eva's laptop, Weckworth swore graphically.

"I'm pulling you out now. You've screwed this one up, Grayson. All because of a woman."

All because of a woman.

Now Adam glanced at the way Eva crossed her legs, the material of her skirt sliding off to the side, giving him a tantalizing view of her knees. It was also because of that woman, he'd explained to Weckworth, that he couldn't leave. Not yet. Not until he had this case wrapped up and he was sure she'd be safe.

"There," Eva said, leaning forward to point at the screen. "See how it did that?"

Yes, Adam did. The moment he opened the file, the computer loaded what appeared to be an intergalactic game of some sort. Yellow stars crisscrossed the screen around the 3-D title *Triumph of the Gladiators.* He pressed the needed buttons to enter. Nothing but a game. And an unsophisticated one at that. A colorful take on one of those video tennis–type games. Except instead of two cursors batting a ball back and forth, a gladiator and an alien tossed fireballs at each other, then deflected them.

He spent the next half hour trying to find a back door to the program, then exited. Nothing. Nothing but a game.

He ran his fingers through his hair and sighed, scanning the title page. Given the simplicity of the game, it couldn't have taken much space on the high-density disk. He exited again and listed the directory. The file of interest took far too much memory for the simple game he'd just played.

He snapped upright.

"What is it?" Eva asked, leaning closer, her breasts brushing his arm.

Adam nearly groaned. His body yearned to forget all this in exchange for losing himself in the intoxicating woman next to him.

"I don't know yet," he said, going back to the title screen.

He sat back and looked long and hard, trying several key combinations that might give him access to what he was convinced was a secret passageway into the program. Nothing.

Next he resorted to clicking the mouse on different areas of the program. He positioned the pointer arrow on the helmet of the gladiator and the game screen vanished.

"Now we're onto something."

He spent the next five minutes urgently entering different key combinations. It wasn't until he had the arrow in the far right-hand corner of the screen, and pressed the control and escape keys simultaneously, that a menu system blipped up that had nothing to do with games, and everything to do with hidden accounting activities.

"Got you, Sheffert," Adam muttered with Eva looking on.

EVA DIDN'T KNOW much about undercover operations, but she knew enough about accounting and the law to spot a phantom ledger. And that's exactly what Adam had pulled up on the Honeycutt account. All the secret transactions made to look clean on her accounts. All the sly little ways to shuffle money around and keep it out of the tax man's hands. And all the crafty distribution of monies and assets to make it appear that Honeycutt owned far less than they actually did. They were all mapped out in front of her like a white-collar criminal's guide to tax evasion.

She rubbed her temples, realizing that the FTC audit on Honeycutt's account she had been preparing for had more to do with this than the simple clerical errors she had been led to believe by Norman Sheffert himself.

"You've got him," she said quietly, slipping her hand to lay against Adam's arm.

His grin was a thousand percent pure Adam Grayson. An alpha male who knew where he stood in the world and knew exactly how to manipulate it for his own purposes. And, Eva realized, he could use those same charming skills on women. While his grin affected her in a more profound way than any of Adam-the-geek's smiles had, she also recognized that Adam-the-alpha would never have broken through the charm-proof barriers she had erected after Bill had walked out on her. No, it had taken nerdy Adam to slip past those. But it was definitely a combination of the two Adams that had made her fall in love with the man next to her.

And she did love him. More profoundly than she'd ever loved any man before him. And, she feared, more acutely than she would love anyone else again.

"Yes, I'd say I definitely have Sheffert by the shorts."

Her hand grew hot where she still touched him, but she didn't remove it. "So, I did end up having what you needed."

The grin faded from Adam's handsome face. Replaced by an intense expression that seemed to say so much more. "Yes. You did end up having what I needed."

With his other hand, he lifted hers from where it rested on his arm and brought it to his mouth. His brown eyes darkened as he pressed her palm against his lips, then nipped at the flesh there. Eva gasped softly, her body humming to life even as he abruptly released her and shut down the computer, slipping the diskette into his front shirt pocket.

"Where are the troops?" he asked.

"Gone. They went to my aunt and uncle's for dinner to celebrate Labor Day. They wanted..." She trailed off, her heartbeat growing heavier with each breath. "They wanted us to go, too, but I bowed out, telling them I wasn't feeling well."

As they stood, the fact that they weren't touching had little effect on the heady currents running between them.

"And are you feeling well?"

"I'm feeling just fine."

ADAM DIDN'T KNOW what it was about this incredible woman that had touched him so. But as he led her to the bedroom, then closed the door and crushed her against him, he knew that she'd touched a place he hadn't allowed anyone even to glimpse before.

Up until now, his life had been a series of undercover assignments, where he switched from identity to identity with the ease of an actor. He had seen the undercover demands as part of his job, his disguises a requirement. Now he questioned whether *he* required the concealment the job provided. He suspected he hadn't been merely doing his job. He had been hiding. Hiding from love. From true commitment. From anyone and everyone who could ever touch his heart and open him up to pain.

Then there was this weekend and Eva. Sultry, earthy, Eva Mavros Burgess. In turns, a competent, independent professional. A caring, dedicated daughter. A promising, loving mother. Then there was the woman he held against his hard length now. The passionate siren who knew what she wanted and knew how to make him want it too. It was her presence, her wit and her uncommon desire that had proved to him that without pain there also could be no true joy.

Odd that he should feel both so acutely now. Pain because he knew he'd soon be losing her. Joy because he had these next few hours to indulge in the wonderful fantasies that had changed during their time together. Dreams that would never be realized to their full extent.

Eva drew slightly away and switched on a small lamp in the corner, filling the room with soft, yellow light.

"I want to see you," she murmured.

Adam smoothed the dark cloud of hair back from her face, then rested a hand against her cheek, drinking in the expression she wore just for him. He slowly brushed his lips over hers, reveling in the way she allowed him to take charge for this one instant. Content to hand him the reins, her lips parted, her sensuous olive green eyes watching him through the fringe of her dark lashes, her body still. Her surrendering of control touched off an overwhelming sense of power to know he had caused this wondrously independent woman to trust him. To give herself to him completely, with no promises.

He drew slightly back, holding her gaze captive, reading in her expression what he knew to be the truth. That there could be no promises. She wasn't ready to commit to him. And he couldn't commit to her. Not in the way she needed him to. No matter how strongly he wished he could. Four days ago he didn't think he'd ever commit to a woman. Now he was faced with a woman carrying another man's child. And living with the aching knowledge that he had nothing to offer either one of them beyond now.

With a low groan, he slid his hand to the back of her head, entwining his fingers in her thick dark hair, tugging on the wavy strands so her neck arched, her mouth tilted upward, her impossibly sexy lips inviting him to take them.

And take them he did. He claimed her mouth with such hunger that he could bury himself within her that moment and explode with the ferocious intensity born of long-denied need. He'd always been the one to take control in a relationship, but though Eva's stillness represented surrender, Adam realized that she was the one in charge of them both. With a word, she could stop his seduction. With a touch, she could take them both further.

His tongue plunged in and out of her mouth, probing the soft flesh of her inner cheek, the smoothness of her teeth, tangling with her tongue, challenging it to come out. He wasn't going any further until she openly invited him to, encouraged him to touch her. Until she let him know with her actions that she wanted him as desperately as he needed her.

The moment she did proved to be one of the sweetest, most defining moments of Adam's life. Eva melted against him, slipping her arms around his waist, opening her mouth to take him in and using her tongue to let him know she needed him as much as he needed her.

He slid his arms over her lush body, running his fingers slowly, intently, down from her shoulders. Pressing a path over the hollow of her back, then grasping the firm flesh of her bottom before crowding her to his erection.

A groan ripped from his throat. He leaned his head back, marveling in the feel of her softness against his hard length. Streaks of fire blasted through his groin and abdomen, stoking a blaze of a different kind already burning in his chest. It was then he knew what he suspected all along. That what was to happen between them now would be much more than sex...it would be the sweet uniqueness of making love. It would be magic.

Dragging his hands back up to her face, he held her still, exploring and claiming her mouth with increased need. A man incapable of probing deeply enough, tasting nearly enough to satisfy.

Eva shoved the material of his shirt up and out of the waist of his slacks until her fingertips touched his overly aware flesh. She drew long lines up and down his back, not quite scratching his skin, but not quite caressing it either. Then she plunged her hands into the waist of his pants and circled her fingers around the band to the front. Adam sucked in a breath when she brushed her knuckles against his stomach, persuaded to loosen his grip on her as she fumbled with his zipper.

Within moments her hot fingers curled around his erection. Holding tight. Making him feel that everything that was him resided there and was hers for the taking. He surged against her grasp and she began a slow up-and-down movement that stoked his fires even higher.

"Eva, I want you...need you," he whispered fiercely against her mouth. "More than I've ever needed anyone else before."

Her eyelids fluttered open. "I'm here, Adam. I'm here."

And that she was. Every delicious inch of her.

Moving his hands from her rear, he ripped at the shoulders of her dress, too impatient to slide out the buttons he had fantasized about undoing with his teeth earlier. Satisfied, he watched the tiny buttons pop out of the stretched buttonholes. Finally her breasts were bare but for a scrap of satin and lace. She reached around and hastily removed her bra, so even that barrier was taken away.

He lowered his head to smother and lave her dark nipples. One, then the other and back again. His hands teasing, squeezing. His mouth suckling, licking and tasting until he heard her breath come in rapid, ragged gasps. He fastened his lips around her right nipple and suckled deeply, then opened his mouth and took in more of her breast even as he dropped his hands back to her waist. Yanking up the hem of her skirt, he sought the panties clinging to her perfectly curved bottom, then eased his fingers inside the elastic. He slowly drew the tip of his index finger along the swollen folds of flesh that protected her until it rested against the tiny, puckered aperture just beyond.

Eva whimpered. She lifted one long leg and wrapped it around him, catching her knee on his hip. She pressed hard against his erection while Adam teased her from the other side, shifting his fingertip and gently parting her silken folds, then dipping his finger into her sweet, hot wetness.

There was pure power in knowing he could make her come apart with his hand. But Adam reminded himself he had already done that. Now he wanted her fully, wanted to bury himself deep inside her, feel her sleek muscles contract around him, pulling him deeper, pleading with him to stay.

Eva eased her hold on his arousal and tunneled her

hands into his hair. She coaxed his mouth up to hers, her hunger a palpable thing.

Slipping his fingers from her dripping sweetness, he yanked at her panties. Eva tugged at the front of his pants until she freed him, the scraps of silk and lace and white cotton dropping to the floor. Scraping his callused palms up her legs until they rested against the backs of her thighs, he boosted her up.

She grasped for his shoulders to steady herself, groaning when her damp fissure rested against his painfully hard erection.

For one long moment their breathing stopped. Their gazes locked as they teetered on the edge of a precipice that, once passed, would mean no going back.

"Are you sure?" he murmured. "Are you sure I won't hurt—"

She pressed her fingers against his lips. "The baby will be fine." Her gaze shifted to his mouth. "And I've never been so sure of anything in my life."

Her whispered words were Adam's unraveling.

She leaned away from him until her fingers barely touched behind his neck, giving him a clear view of her luscious body where it was bared down to the dress bunched around her waist. Her breasts were tight and round, her nipples puckered and damp from his attentions. Then she shifted her hips and all coherent thought scattered to the four winds.

Cupping her bottom in his hands, Adam gently, slowly lifted her, then brought her down on his arousal inch by torturous inch, pausing to give her time to accommodate him, plunging ahead once her gasps stopped. Then, finally, he was completely surrounded by everything that was Eva, the sensations ripping through him the closest he had come to heaven.

Slowly, he moved them toward the bed a few feet away and lay her down on the sheets. He thrust deeply inside her and she threw her head back and moaned, a sound that wove around him, beckoned to him in a way he was unable to resist.

Grasping her hips, he thrust into her again, then again, and yet again, each plunge heightening the emotions pulsing though him. Pushing them up, further and further, taking him to the brink of climax, then slowly, bringing them back down as he evened the rhythm of their lovemaking.

Releasing his hold on the pliant flesh of her hips, he flattened his hands across her abdomen, then brought his thumbs together at her navel. She stilled, her breathing ragged, her stomach muscles contracting beneath his touch. She watched him through the dark fringe of her lashes as he slid his thumbs downward. He halted at the spot between belly button and the dark dusky triangle below. He reminded himself of the special meaning of what lay beneath her silky, slightly rounded flesh. How he yearned at that moment that the life growing within her was a result of their lovemaking, hers and his.

Eva shifted restlessly and he continued his downward path until his thumbs rested against her slick, tangled hair.

She gasped and stopped moving. Adam shifted his hips slightly to the right, then to the left, parting her soft folds until she was exposed to him, pink and engorged. He pressed a thumb purposefully down on the silky nub, slowly rubbing it in small circles.

Eva arched her back and dissolved with a series of shudders and gasps, her climax rippling through her. Her spasms traveled from her to him, where Adam had stilled, but kept up the caress of his thumb, drawing her moment out, carrying her along. But instead of the orchestrating role he expected to play, her slick, sleek muscles tightened around him. And the pleasure at having brought her to orgasm swept through him. He surged into her, deeper, and yet deeper again, following on the heels of her climax. Energy quaked through him, robbing him of breath, of movement, for a moment that seemed to stretch into eternity.

Eva dropped back to the sheets, her rosy skin glistening with perspiration, the muted light from the lamp in the corner imprinting her abdomen with the shadow of an iron post. Adam eased his body from the taut, straight position that had allowed the wondrous sensations to rip through him.

For long moments, he stayed motionless, wanting to put into words what he felt, yet fearing no words could do his emotions justice. Instead, he watched Eva, waiting for her to catch her breath, anticipating the moment when she would come back to him for more. And she did. The ceiling fan stirred her dark, damp hair as she looked at him, need burning deep in her eyes.

Adam groaned as he hardened all over again, urged on by the tightening of her muscles.

This time there was no controlled manipulation, no conscious effort to please. Instead, when Adam thrust into her, his movements growing faster and harder, Eva's moans coming louder and sweeter, it was in a selfish quest for fulfillment only complete surrender to his emotions could give. And when the white light that had filled him at the onset of their lovemaking began showing shoots of wild, vivid reds, Adam knew it would be unlike anything he had ever experienced before…or would likely experience again.

His muscles grew rigid, the thunder of climax clutching his entire body. Adam gripped her hips, holding her still, absorbing her pleasure, communicating his own to her.

Slowly, the shock waves ebbed. Adam slid his hands

up her glistening body, extending her arms, then joined his fingers with hers above her head.

"I love you," he murmured. He thought his saying the words should surprise him, but he was helpless to do anything but let the truth show. Wonder at the freedom with which it filled him. No matter how vain the words.

Releasing one of her hands, he smoothed the tangled hair from her face. It was impossible to believe there was a greater sight than her serene, ethereal smile, something sweeter than the emotion-filled kiss she gave him.

"I love you more," she murmured.

Her eyes were too bright, too luminous. Adam followed the trail of a tear as it slid down her cheek. A profound, answering sadness tore through his chest. He rested his palm against her face and wiped the dampness away, wishing he could say something to ease her pain...to ease his own. But nothing could reverse the knowledge that despite all they had shared, all that bound them together, they might never be together like this again.

11

ADAM LAY AWAKE into the wee hours of the morning, unable to give himself over to the forgetfulness sleep might offer. Eva was curled against him, her warmth welcome despite the sultry, heavy heat of the night. He caressed her bare arm, amazed that he wanted to wake her yet again and indulge in her sweet, hot body. Marvel in the emotions he now knew she felt for him as strongly as he felt them for her. But after endless hours of passionate exploration, he suspected she needed rest, evidenced by her soft snores.

Turning his head to look at her in the dim light of her moon, he pushed the hair back from her damp face, then pressed a gentle kiss to her forehead. Oh but she tasted good. He kept his lips against her skin for long moments, then closed his eyes, thinking that a life filled with nights like this were a very tempting proposition indeed.

An hour or so before, he'd heard a car pull up, and listened as Eva's parents, grandmother and brother made their way into the house, their voices quiet, spurts of laughter floating to him on the thick night air.

Now the house was silent but for the ticking of a large grandfather clock in the main foyer and the hushed whirl of the ceiling fan. Adam shifted Eva slightly to remove his arm where it had begun to fall asleep. Her soft, unconscious objection surprised him, as did her sigh when he cuddled her close again.

Adam had never been needed before. Not in this

way. Not by a woman who seemed to need no one. And for a man who had never needed anyone himself, he found it all too easy to need Eva and everything she offered. Everything he'd never had. Love. Family. Commitment.

With his free hand, he rubbed his forehead. He wasn't surprised by how easily he had become a part of Eva and her family's lives in just a few days. It was part and parcel of his job. But it was amazing that they had become so much a part of his.

Still, he seriously had to question the solidity of such a statement. The past four days were unlike any he'd ever experienced in many ways. Both wonderful and daunting. But could he trust the peace he found here when everything about the time loomed surreal and isolated? As if part of a disjointed dream that couldn't possibly be real?

He supposed the source for his doubts sprouted from the deception on which so much of what he felt now was built. His accepting Eva's offer when he was already playing the role of Adam the socially challenged accountant. His attraction to her when he should have kept her at arm's length. The ingenuous way members of her family had welcomed him, leaving him feeling a part of them no matter how much he resisted.

And most puzzling, the longing deep within him to protect and love the child Eva carried even though it wasn't his. Lord, but he recognized that his yearning might even be because the child wasn't his, due in part to his own parentless upbringing. And due even more to his all-encompassing love for Eva.

Movement in the hall caught his attention. Adam picked up the clock from the bedside table and squinted at it. Four-thirty. He knew Tolly wasn't going in to work today because a storm was due to roll in later that morning. Still, the man could have his own internal alarm that made him get up at the same hour every morning. Adam put the clock back down and gently repositioned Eva so he could get up, this time ignoring her soft protests. After the ransacking of Eva's room, then the theft of her laptop, Adam couldn't allow himself to trust that the early-morning sounds came from Tolly or anyone else in the house.

Slipping into the itchy polyester slacks that had marked his time here, he stood up and zipped them, then silently headed in the direction of the door.

The sharp report of what he immediately identified as a gunshot ripped through the night.

"Damn."

Throwing open the door, Adam distantly registered Eva's calling out to him even as he tore down the hall, then the steps, emerging onto the front porch to make out two dark silhouettes standing some ten feet apart in the yard.

"Don't you move, you stinkin' thief!" Adam recognized Tolly's heavily accented voice. Adam discerned him as the figure closer to him. He descended the stairs, the grass cool and damp beneath his bare feet.

Tolly Mavros was holding a gun.

"What in the hell are you doing," Adam asked, reaching out and snatching the firearm from Tolly's hands. A quick look verified that it was indeed his own gun, missing from Eva's room the day before. "This is mine. How did you get it?"

Tolly waved at him impatiently. "When I saw it on the floor of Eva's room after the break-in, I thought maybe the intruder left it behind." He shrugged irritably. "So I took it."

Adam grimaced. It seemed Tolly had seen far more than Eva's divorce papers. He remembered how the wily Greek had clutched a bunched up towel in his hands throughout the aftermath of the break-in. Only, the towel hadn't been all he'd been holding.

"You stick with oysters and I'll take care of any shooting that needs to be done, okay?" Adam said. It rankled that Tolly had taken the gun right out from under his own nose. The reminder of just how far he'd let his guard down bothered him.

The figure ten feet away started to move. Adam aimed the weapon at him, refocusing on the matter at hand.

"Oh no you don't, buddy," he said. "You're not going anywhere. Maybe Tolly here couldn't hit you, but rest assured, I've got very good aim."

He stepped closer to the dark figure, the light from the full moon reflecting off the fishing lures hooked above the rim of the hat the person wore. As on the two other occasions he'd seen the suspect—first at the rest area, then at the warehouse the day before—he had never gotten a good look at his face.

Adam stopped and waved the gun. "Take the hat off."

"Shoot him," Tolly said, appearing at his side. He jostled Adam's arm with his elbow. "Shoot the son of a bitch."

Adam fought a smile. Good thing he'd taken the pistol away from the hotheaded man.

The suspect slipped off the hat, crumpling it in his shaking hands.

"Oliver!" Eva gasped from somewhere behind him.

"Pinney." Adam sighed.

Now that the hat was off, it wasn't difficult to recognize the wiry-haired accountant who had launched Adam's entire investigation when the high-strung man had spilled more than he'd intended in John Weckworth's office four weeks ago.

"Now that you know who I am, who are you?" Pinney whimpered.

"Field Agent Grayson of the FBI." Adam grimaced, then dropped his gun to his side. "Well, I suppose I should be relieved your body isn't polluting a river somewhere, Pinney," he said. "But right now I can't help feeling disappointed that we can't get Sheffert for conspiracy to murder."

"That's not funny, Mr....Agent Grayson," Pinney said in his whiny little voice.

"Agent Grayson? FBI?" Tolly repeated. He looked over his shoulder at where Adam guessed Eva was. "What the hell is going on here? What is he talking about?"

Adam shook his head, keeping his focus on Pinney. How had this *real* geek ever summoned the guts to do what he'd done over the past four days?

"Then change my mind, Pinney," Adam said. "And you can start with why you staged your own disappearance."

"I...I had to go underground. I told you Sheffert would have me filed away permanently."

Adam narrowed his eyes. "We told you we'd protect you."

"Protect me? You call making me stay on that job until I got evidence, protecting me?"

"Yes, I do. Because once you produced the evidence, Sheffert would never be a worry to you again."

Eva finally moved into view on the other side of Adam, her arms wrapped around her upper body. "That's why you were so nervous around the office. It wasn't just the audit...."

Pinney's finger shook as he pointed it at her. "You would be, too, if you knew your life was in danger."

Two figures rushed from the trees bordering the

yard. Adam reached out to prevent Tolly from charging them. "They're with me," he said.

The two agents grabbed Pinney's arms and cuffed him despite his high-pitched protests.

"Where in the hell were you guys?" Adam asked, sliding the pistol barrel first into the back waistband of his slacks. "Looks like I had better backup in Tolly here than you two."

Eva's father hmmphed.

"Get a grip, Grayson," one of the agents said. "We were keeping an eye on the situation. The suspect didn't get any closer than he is now before this old man shot out of the house and started firing. We were assessing the situation before deciding how to proceed."

Eva slipped her hand into the crook of Adam's arm. He wondered at the warmth that filled him even in the midst of the present situation.

"Yes, well, Pinney had better thank somebody that Tolly isn't a good shot."

"You need me," Pinney whined.

"Uh-uh. Not anymore I don't. Last night we found the files you were after." Adam rubbed his chin. "Of course, the case would be stronger if we had you to testify that you set up the accounts for Sheffert. If, indeed, that is the case."

Eva squeezed his arm. "What are you saying?"

Adam glanced at her, loving the way the light of her moon played on her enchanting face. "Oh, just that after thinking about the files we reviewed last night, I suspect Sheffert might not be the only one involved in this. Pinney might not be the innocent victim he pretends, but a coconspirator. And if he hadn't cracked when the FBI questioned him during the open audit, he would never have needed to cover the tracks he'd laid out leading to Sheffert and to others in the office that were involved." He watched Pinney's chin drop to his chest. "That's why he disappeared. That's why we also found the safe in Sheffert's office open long after he'd already left for the weekend. He hadn't left it open for Alice to put disks away, but rather to give her and Pinney access to the safe and the disks so they could clean them up.

"But when you got to the disks before they did, Pinney knew he needed to get them back before anyone got a look at them."

Eva pulled her hair away from her face with her free hand. "Alice? You think she's in on this, too? But how can you be so sure Pinney's involved, and not a victim, like he said?"

"I'm not, but all accountants have their own little ways of doing things," Adam told her, "leaving the equivalent of fingerprints all over the ledgers they create by the way they enter the data, manipulate it. Having been stuck in Pinney's office for the past three weeks, I got all too familiar with the way our friend here does business. And after seeing the ghost ledgers and the way he hid them in a computer game, I knew he was actively, earnestly involved. A partner, not a victim.

"At any rate, if I'm wrong about my assumptions, we'll find out soon enough. Pinney cracks wide open under pressure, so I'm sure he'll tell us all what we need to know."

He looked at her meaningfully, longingly. "What matters now is that it's over."

"Oh." Eva whispered the one-word response, then slowly took her hand from his arm as if realizing it didn't belong there.

Suddenly, she looked all too vulnerable, and all too hurt. *It's over.* Adam realized that his comment could easily apply to their own tentative relationship. He had to use every shred of control he had, not to reach out to reassure her. Because the simple fact was, the statement *did* apply to their unconventional relationship as well.

"I thought Adam was a stockbroker," Eva's mother said, breaking the awkward silence.

THE PERVASIVE RESIGNATION that claimed every one of Eva's muscles helped her deal with the barrage of questions with feigned calm. In truth, she wanted to be with Adam, who had stayed out front with the two other agents, while she ushered her baffled family into the house to face the tedious task of explaining everything to them.

"Here, have some tea," her mother said, placing a generous cup in front of her. Eva leaned her head against her hand and smiled. Why was it that even at the worst of times, her mother always somehow managed to put something on the table?

"You knew this Adam, he was an undercover agent?" her father asked, sipping on his own Greek coffee in a tiny porcelain cup.

"No. Yes. I found out yesterday afternoon."

"And he's not your husband."

Eva dropped her gaze to her lap. "No, Papa, he's not."

For long moments no one said anything. Eva couldn't bring herself to care about anything but the fact that Adam would be leaving now. He would disappear from her life as quickly as he had entered it.

Is that what he had intended all along? Eva didn't believe it. Not after what they shared together last night, not after he'd said he loved her.

And she knew he did. As surely as she knew the deep pain at the thought of losing him grew out of her love for him, too.

"Your Bill...is he dead?" her grandmother asked.

That brought a watery smile to Eva's face. She reached out and patted her grandmother's pale hand. "No, Yaya, Bill is still alive. We're just…divorced."

Her father hmmphed and leaned back in his chair. But instead of avoiding his gaze, Eva looked directly at him.

"And the baby? It is his…Bill's?" he asked.

"Yes," she said quietly. "My pregnancy is the reason Bill asked for a divorce. You see, we agreed when we married that we wouldn't have children."

"Not have—"

Eva's mother entered the room carrying a tray of toast. "Tolly, stop it right now. Let the child speak, for God's sake."

Eva cleared her tight throat. "When Mama called to tell me you were ill—" her mother shrugged innocently when her father glared at her "—I just couldn't bring myself to tell you I was divorced from a man you hadn't even met. I knew it hurt you all that I married away from home and without your blessing. And, well, since I didn't know how ill you were, I didn't want to lay that in your lap as well."

"And Adam?" her grandmother asked. "You are…involved with him?"

"No." Eva's cheeks burned with the lie, but she couldn't bear to share with them how…close she and Adam had become over the past few days. And anyway, before she brought him to Louisiana, they had been little more than associates.

Her father sat forward. "For three nights you sleep with him in the same room in my house, you call him husband, and yet you say you're not involved with him?" He paused. "Okay, two nights. One night he slept on the porch."

Eva smiled sadly. "We're not involved in the way I suspect you hope we are." She wrapped her cold fin-

gers around her cup. "I am not going to marry Adam
Papa."

"Why not?" he asked. "He is a good man. He woul_
be a good protector, a good father to your son."

"Or daughter," her mother said.

Eva tightly closed her eyes. "I'm not going to marry
Adam," she said more loudly. "So just drop it, okay?"

"Drop it? What is this, drop it?" Tolly said.

Her mother quickly explained the meaning of the
words in Greek, then her father nodded and went silent.

"Do you love him, *ayapee mou?*" Her grandmother
broke the silence. All gazes shifted to Eva's face.

She briefly closed her eyes. "Yes, I do."

Her father slapped his hand on the table. "And he
loves you, so it's settled. You'll be married tomorrow
by Pappa Kostas in Morgan City."

Eva put her teacup on the table with a dull thud.
"Papa, this is not the Middle Ages. And this is not
Greece where you can just order me around as if I'm a
mindless child whose only duty is to obey you. I don't
need to be married to have a baby." She pleaded for
him to understand, but suddenly recognized that it
was enough for her to say the words. "Why can't you
just accept my decision? Respect me as I do you?"

"Respect? This is what you call respect?"

Eva started to rise from the table. "You're determined to chase me away again, aren't you? If I can't
abide by your rules, then you'd just as soon I wasn't in
your sight, isn't that right? Let me go back to New Jersey and live my life in some sort of archaic exile to return only for vacations where you can remind me all
over again why I'm undeserving of your love."

She drew herself up. "Well, I'm telling you right
now. I've decided I'm not going anywhere. Even
though Adam won't be a part of my life...our lives

e's made me realize some very important things. And one of them is that I love my family and I want to be near them. Near Mama, Yaya, Pete, and yes, even you, Papa. No matter how difficult you make it." She smoothed her hands over her slightly rounded stomach through her nightgown. "I'm going to be staying on in Belle Rivage to raise my child."

The room was awkwardly silent after her small speech. But Eva felt better than she had in a long, long time, despite the sadness clinging to her like the humid air. Her grandmother was smiling, but her mother watched her father's angry face, her own full of hope that he would say something to make everything right. Deep down, Eva wished for the same. But she finally realized that even if her father said nothing, it wouldn't matter. She was who she was, and he was the same.

"Good," he said gruffly moments later.

"Good?" Eva's chest tightened.

He waved his hand as if shooing her away. "Yes, good. I never liked that you left here, Eva. And I'm sorry you felt I'm the one who forced you away."

Through her tears, her father was a gruff, lovable blur.

"But you should still marry Adam."

Eva's throat was thick with emotion. "I can't, Papa. He's not the father of this child. I can't ask him to take on the responsibility. No matter what may have happened between us this past weekend." She started from the room. "I won't."

With her words she left out one important truth. Adam hadn't offered to take on the responsibility of her...or her baby.

ADAM HAD NO IDEA leaving Eva would be so difficult. In the past four days he'd seen her transform from the ice queen he had once thought her, into a dedicated daughter in a tight-knit Greek-American family. And finally into a sensual, loving woman who could make everything in the world all right with just one of her heartwarming smiles, one passionate touch.

As Adam packed his things, he found it odd that nowhere in his thoughts of her was the image of Eva wearing that string bikini. No. Now looming far sexier in his mind was Eva and her floral dresses, her olive green eyes full of passion as she looked at him while they made love.

Damn, he'd gotten himself in deep this time. But would the feelings burgeoning in his chest for Eva Mavros Burgess last after a week away from her? A bothersome voice shouted yes, they would. But things had happened too quickly for him to trust that voice. To trust himself not to hurt Eva, her family and her child if he woke up one day and realized his love for her was little more than an overdose of lust, or an almost obsessive thirst for the forbidden.

Anyway, he had to leave. He was scheduled on the next flight out to Jersey to pull in Norman Sheffert and Alice Turley for questioning. Combined with Pinney's forthcoming confession he had no doubt everything would be sewn up by the day's end.

Would he come back?

He knew the answer even before he thought it. *No.* It wouldn't be fair to her or her family to drag out the inevitable. And the inevitable was that he didn't belong here.

Besides, he thought as he closed his duffel bag, she hadn't asked him to stay. Chances were, she didn't think they had what it took to make it beyond tomorrow any more than he did. As accountants, both of them knew half of new business ventures failed within the first year. Even with the best of guidance and everything on their side when they started out. It wasn't any different in marriage, if the current divorce rates were anything to go by. He'd never done anything impulsive in his life. And he'd hazard a guess that Eva hadn't either. But their making love fell solidly in the impulse category. They had come together knowing full well there would be no promises when the sun rose.

He glanced up and through the window, finding the hot September sun doing exactly that. And he was completely convinced he was doing the right thing. Well, almost convinced. Okay, he had a strong feeling his walking away was right.

Damn, why couldn't he be sure?

At any rate, his future was already decided. An hour earlier, he'd called Deputy Chief John Weckworth to fill him in on the peculiar circumstances surrounding the case and to have him put a tail on Sheffert and his secretary. At the end of their conversation, Weckworth had told him of another assignment. Adam had taken it. After he wrapped this case up, he was going to close up his apartment in New Jersey, then catch a flight to Little Rock, Arkansas, where his next case waited.

"Adam?"

Every muscle in his body tensed at the sound of Eva's voice from the open door. Picking up his briefcase and duffel, he turned toward her.

She released her bottom lip where she had caught it between her teeth. Adam wanted to groan. The urge to pull her to him and kiss away her pain—and his own—was overwhelming. But her stance well across the room clearly stated that such a move would be unwise.

"Are you ready?" she asked quietly.

"Yes. Yes, I am."

She gestured toward the hall with those wonderfully long, slender hands. "I already told my parents you wouldn't be saying goodbye. I, uh, thought it would be better for them that way." She scanned his face. "And you."

He nodded, a part of him regretting that he wouldn't be offering any explanation to her family, telling them how much he had enjoyed the past few days with them, but he knew it was for the best. No sense acting as if they might see each other again. Because they wouldn't.

"Come on. I'll walk you out."

Being so close to Eva, and not being able to touch her, to tell her how very much last night meant to him, or to promise her everything if she'd only let him stay was the most difficult thing Adam had ever done. He followed her down the hall, then the stairs. He ordered himself not to watch the way her dress swung around her legs, or eye the enticing curve of her neck as they stepped out onto the porch. But he did both, needing to capture at least that image of her before he left.

She turned to him, her dark eyebrows drawn together. "How are you going to get back to Jersey?"

"Are you offering to drive me?" he asked, smiling, and wishing he hadn't said anything when a ray of hope flashed in her eyes. He forced himself to look away. "I'll be flying from New Orleans."

"But I thought...oh." Her hand shook as she tucked her hair behind her ear. "Your not being able to fly was just part of the assignment."

"Yes."

She gave him a small smile.

He eyed her drawn face, wishing for all the world that he didn't have to hurt her. That he didn't have to hurt himself. But knowing it was better now than later. "And you? When will you be going back?"

"I won't," she said softly. "At least not to stay. Of course, I'll have to sell my house and settle everything

in New Jersey first, but I'm going to come back here."
She gestured toward the house. "A lot of what you said
to me on the boat the other night made sense. I've decided I've done enough running and that I should just
stick things out here. For my sake—" she ran her fingers down her abdomen "—and for my baby's."

He nodded. "Good."

She stared at him in a way that made him feel uneasy. "That's exactly what my father said."

"A smart man, your father."

Her answering laugh was a little stronger than her
previous one. "You would say that."

They shared a moment jam-packed with awkward-
ness and tension. Caught up in the emotion of the moment, swept away by passion, neither of them quite
knew what to say now.

A car pulled up into the circular driveway and
parked behind Eva's Mercedes.

She flicked it a quick glance. "Well, I guess I should
say goodbye and let you get on your way. You have
work to do." She lifted her eyes to him, peering at him
from beneath the thick fringe of her dark lashes. Adam
felt like groaning all over again. "Goodbye, Adam,"
she whispered.

Hesitantly stepping toward him, she dropped her
gaze, intent on kissing him on the cheek. But Adam
wasn't having any of that. Dropping his bags, he cradled her face in his hands and met her lips head-on.

Her eyes blinked up to gaze into his as he slanted his
mouth against hers, prying her lips apart to dip his
tongue inside for one last, torturous taste of her mouth,
her essence, the very things that made Eva so special.
Instead of pulling away, she plunged her tongue
against his, forcing it back into his mouth, her eyes flut-
tering closed as she pressed her hand to the back of his

neck, pulling him closer, tempting him with the feel of her luscious body against his.

Then it was over and she stepped back, her cheeks flushed, her eyes overly bright, her fingers lightly touching her lips.

"Goodbye, Eva."

She nodded. He turned to walk down the steps and out of her life.

EVA MOVED to the top of the steps, wanting to call out to Adam, to beg him to come back, but she could do nothing more than hold back her tears as the car drove out of sight. Slowly, she sat down on the top step, smoothing her dress over her knees and giving vent to the sobs clogging her throat.

He was gone. Although Adam Grayson had only graced her life for such a short time—first as the endearing, sexy geek Adam Gardner with the taped-together glasses, then as the megawatt charmer who touched her in all the right places, including her heart—Eva felt nothing would ever be the same again.

Behind her the hinges on the screen door squeaked. Eva quickly swiped at her tears and lifted her chin, thinking her mother had followed her out. She flattened her hands on the porch and sat forward, waiting for the questions that would inevitably follow Adam's departure. Instead, she was met with silence. Shifting her glance to the spot next to her, she found that her father was slowly sitting down.

"Adam, he's going to arrest this other man, your boss, no?"

She nodded numbly. "Yes."

Left unsaid was the question of his possible return.

A fresh bout of tears blurred her vision. She sat stiffly, waiting for her father to say he told her so, or tell her it wasn't too late to go after Adam. But he did neither. He merely sat there with her, staring in the direction Adam's car had gone. Then he reached out and covered her hand with his big, callused one. Showing her, in the only way he knew how, that he was there for her. And always would be.

"Tomorrow we go out on the boat," he said quietly.

Eva instinctively leaned into him and wept.

12

FOUR MONTHS LATER, Adam stared out the window of a downtown Chicago skyscraper, watching the blinding white snowflakes snake around the building and drift to the ground far below. Upon leaving Louisiana and wrapping up the Sheffert case like a Christmas gift, he'd closed his apartment in Edison, New Jersey, and gone on to Little Rock, Arkansas, where he completed his next assignment. After that, he had asked that he not be given any undercover work for a while. Weckworth had honored his request and sent him out on two intense open criminal audits, as part of a team Weckworth labeled his Forensic Accounting Combat Unit. They were the elite of the elite, taking apart the books of megamillion-dollar companies and following long, tedious trails that left other accountants cold.

Lord, but that's exactly how Adam felt. Cold. Not even Weckworth's offer last week of an assignment in Hawaii had done anything to warm him.

What did offer a new dimension to his life was that he'd called the foster parents he'd left behind so long ago, inspired mostly by the look at his life Eva had made him take that night on her father's boat. And the need to right the wrongs of his past. Wrongs made blamelessly, but made nonetheless.

It had surprised him that Carol Richmond had immediately recognized his voice, though ten years had passed since he'd last spoken to her. And the memory of her and Dan's warm reaction to him when he'd visited them in Luckey, Ohio, for Thanksgiving, touched him still. What had begun as an overnight visit stretched into three days during which he'd caught up on all the happenings since he'd joined the FBI. Not the least of which was that he had six nieces and nephews. *Six nieces and nephews.* He hadn't even been aware that others had thought of him as a brother. Now he was an uncle.

What he wouldn't have given to be able to tell them another addition to the untraditional family was on the way.

He owed Eva for providing the thread that had mended that gaping hole in his life. And he might have offered to honor that debt. If only another, greater, aching hole hadn't stopped him.

Last month he'd called the accounting firm renamed Logan and Brace after Sheffert's indictment and asked for Eva, only to be told she had resigned. He knew she would be moving back to Louisiana. He just hadn't realized it would be so quickly. And until he knew exactly what he wanted, he didn't dare contact her at her family's house. It wouldn't be fair to either of them.

What he would have said had she been in New Jersey, he didn't know. He still wasn't sure what had happened between them in Louisiana. What he did know was that by now she would be heavy with the child she would bear in a couple of months. And that he missed her. Missed sharing what was a first in her life.

More than likely, he would have asked to see her. To see with his own eyes that she was okay. To examine the emotions untouched since he'd left her behind in Belle Rivage to see if they indeed had stood the test of time.

Only he already knew that they had. Not a morning went by that he didn't wake up, yearning to reach out and touch her. Not a meal was served that he didn't remember the sight of her sitting across from him, staring in horror at whatever her grandmother had put on her plate. And not a river, lake or even a rain puddle failed to remind him of the night on the boat when he'd stoked the passion within her, then completely unleashed it so they came together in a way that filled his nights with dreams, his heart with yearning.

"Grayson, you coming to lunch or not?" fellow agent O'Brien asked him from the door.

Adam slowly turned, wondering if Eva missed him half as much as he missed her. Wondering if he'd ever be able to repair the hole that gaped even wider with each moment that passed.

EVA LET the screen door slap closed behind her, then stopped to rub the small of her back. Eight months and some three weeks pregnant and she felt as if somebody had strapped a fifty-pound cement bag around her waist. She moved her fingers slowly from her back to her front, marveling at her girth, wondering how her stomach could be so rock-hard. In awe that the baby that moved around incessantly would soon join her and her family.

She pulled her sweater closer. While February temperatures in the bayous of Louisiana didn't get near the freezing temperatures in the north, they hovered between fifty and sixty degrees. The thick humidity made it feel warmer, but Eva wasn't taking any chances. She usually wore a thick pair of leggings, a long jersey shirt and bulky sweater whenever she went to the warehouse. Which was at least once a day to use up some of the restless energy she felt. To ease the pain that even now pierced her heart.

Every day she walked the path from house to warehouse. And every day she thought about Adam. Wondered how he was doing. Imagined him on assignment somewhere buried up to his ears in accounting ledgers.

And she remembered those few sultry days last summer when they had fallen in love.

For days after he left, she'd cried at the drop of a hat. Now… Well, now she struggled to channel those special feelings Adam had awakened in her toward her baby. She missed Adam. Terribly. But it was difficult to focus on what she couldn't have, when what she could have demanded her attention nearly every moment of every day.

Eva emerged from the moss-covered oaks and stared at the warehouse, her restlessness more acute than ever. Mavros Seafood had closed for the season two months ago. But now her father, her brother, Pete, and the employees that were more friends than co-workers, milled around, readying the equipment for the start of a new season. Eva smiled as they uncovered the boat. Then the smile eased from her face as she saw a larger boat next to it.

That's odd. She stepped closer, eyeing the long, narrow sailboat moored to the other side of the dock nearer the bayou.

Jimmy hurried out of the warehouse, newly oiled chain hanging from his shoulder.

"What is that?" Eva called out to him, gesturing toward the handsome schooner.

Jimmy shrugged and kept moving. "Don't know."

She frowned, watching him take the chain to the fishing boat and hand it to her father.

"Eva?" Pete called to her from the door of the warehouse. "Something came for you this morning. It's in the office."

Her gaze lingered on her brother. Her return to live permanently in Belle Rivage had brought on more than the obvious changes in the Mavros family. Papa seemed to have mellowed in a way she never would have thought possible. She guessed it might be because his first grandchild was due any day now. But she sensed it went deeper than that and occasionally she even felt it was her return home that had inspired the change in him.

Then there was Pete. Eva smiled, wondering at the shift in his demeanor. No longer the shadow looming behind Papa, he had finally stood up to Tolly Mavros and even now was building two boats by special request on a piece of family land nearby. He'd agreed to help Papa out from time to time, but he'd made it clear he was going to follow no one's dream but his own. And Papa had not only accepted—however grudgingly—Pete's decision, but Eva secretly believed he was proud of his son.

She shivered. Pete had said something had come for her. What could it be? Why hadn't it been delivered to the house?

As she ducked inside the brightly lit interior of the warehouse, she knew that the something waiting for her couldn't have anything to do with her old job. She'd resigned from Sheffert, Logan and Brace last autumn, with the sale of her house coming soon after. She'd heard from the gossip mill at the firm that Oliver Pinney, Norman Sheffert and Alice Turley were indeed the ones behind the elaborate money-laundering scheme Adam had uncovered, and they were due to stand trial in the spring. Certainly the FBI wasn't contacting her to appear in court?

Leaving the office door open, she stepped to her desk. A desk her father had ordered for her and had had delivered a couple of weeks earlier. Though Eva intended to pursue her accounting career—and had tested the waters in nearby towns, already receiving two offers—after the baby was born, her father was adamant that she also play a role in the business.

"Family," he told her, patting her stomach with his callused hand.

Family, Eva thought now, eyeing a small, rectangular package on her desk.

Her fingers trembling for a reason she couldn't understand, she picked up the plain box, searching it for a return address. There was none. Also evident was that there was no postmark. No indication it had been mailed at all, but likely hand-delivered.

She slipped the top open.

Her heart skipped a beat.

Nestled in some sort of slinky green material were eyeglasses. She took them out to find they weren't just any glasses, but Adam's taped-together glasses. Her throat closed painfully and she slid out the two scraps of material. They were part of a two-piece, very skimpy, very naughty bathing suit.

"Hello, Eva."

The low, achingly familiar sound of the voice hummed through her. For long moments she stood, her back to the door, her eyes tightly closed, unable to believe it could possibly be Adam.

But she needed to know.

She slowly turned toward the voice, clutching the items in her hands as if they could protect her from some unnamed threat. But when she saw his tall, engaging body filling the doorway, she burst into tears. And he turned into one big, endearing blur.

Instantly, he was in front of her and gathering her in his arms. Arms she had longed to feel around her for so long. Arms that were strong, yet gentle, and oh so wonderful to be held by.

"Shh," he whispered, his breath stirring the hair

over her ear. "It's all right now." She felt his deep swallow. "At least I hope it will be."

He smelled of soap and a subtle woodsy cologne, the texture of his flannel shirt soft under her cheek. "Adam—"

"Shh," he said again, rubbing his hands over her arms as if she needed warming. If only he knew just being near him again, just touching him, made her warmer than she could almost bear.

His hands hesitated, then slipped to her sides. Eva took a deep, steadying breath and moved slightly away, her gaze fastening to his. But he wasn't looking at her face. He was looking at her swollen belly.

"May I?" he asked with a rough whisper.

She slowly nodded.

As his hands spanned her stomach, feeling the baby within, she drew in a sharp breath as suppressed emotion started swirling in her chest, growing until she almost felt pain. The awe on his handsomely chiseled face touched her so deeply she feared the tears scalding her cheeks might never stop.

"Is he…she, okay?"

She offered a watery smile. "She's fine."

He lifted his eyebrows and she nodded again. Yes. An ultrasound revealed months ago that her baby was a girl.

"Adam—"

He lifted a finger and pressed it against her mouth. "Shh," he repeated.

Eva grew impatient with longing. She needed to know why he had returned. Why he looked better than any man had a right to. And if…if he was going to stay.

"Eva, I have some things to tell you," he murmured, his brown eyes holding hers. "And I don't want you to say anything until I'm done." He scanned her from hair to chin. "Okay?"

She nodded, suddenly incapable of words.

"I need you to know I never meant to hurt you." He dragged in a breath that told her he was struggling for control. "I can hurt myself to hell and back. I don't care. But the thought that I hurt you…it's something I'll never forgive myself for."

She opened her mouth to speak. To tell him it didn't matter. They'd hurt each other—

"I'm not done yet."

She swallowed back all the words crowding her throat, all the emotion mending her broken heart.

His gaze was penetrating. "Five months ago, when I left you, I did so with honorable intentions." His fingers closed over her upper arms, accelerating her heartbeat. He made a bitter sound of self-loathing. "I thought…I knew I didn't have anything to offer you. I couldn't be the man you needed—the father your daughter needed."

Eva bit her bottom lip hard thinking Adam Grayson would never know how very much he had to offer.

"But my intentions weren't honorable at all. They were driven by cowardice. Everything had happened so fast. I couldn't trust how I felt about you, Eva. I couldn't trust that you could love me. Not the way I loved—love—you, because I couldn't trust myself."

His gaze slipped to her mouth. For a moment he appeared to consider kissing her. He groaned.

"There hasn't been a day over the past five months that I haven't called myself a fool. Told myself I deserved to hurt the way I did." His voice caught. "Until I realized I wasn't only hurting myself. I was hurting you. And that's one thing I can never forgive myself for."

Eva snuggled into the cradle of his arms, yearning for him to stop talking and just hold her, yet needing to hear what he had to say. "Adam—"

"I'm not done."

Smiling despite her tears, she rubbed her cheek against his shirt, her hands pressed tightly against his back. Each of his words were like a salve to her battered soul.

"What I'm trying to say, Eva, is…if you can forgive me…if you'll have me…I want to adopt that precious baby you're carrying…I want you to…I need you to marry me. Now. Tonight. Next week." He dropped to one knee and urgently coaxed her to meet his gaze. "I don't care when. Name the date. Any date. I've taken a supervisory position in the New Orleans office, so I'm not going anywhere anytime soon." He searched her face. "Say anything, but please, don't say it's too late. Don't tell me I've ruined my chances by leaving you."

The air froze in Eva's lungs. Her body refused to move. All she could do was wonder at the pain and uncertainty and hope that darkened Adam's passionate brown eyes. And marvel at the fact that even now, as huge as she was, as uncomfortable, all she wanted to do was lead him up to her room where they could continue where they'd left off. To make love to him in all the ways she had fantasized about for the past months.

She cleared her throat, fighting the need to pull him to his feet. "Is that your boat outside?"

His puzzled expression nearly made her smile.

"Yes, it is."

She held up the naughty bathing suit. "And this?"

A slow, devilish grin spread across his face. "The last thing that's needed to make my fantasy complete until the baby's born." He laid his head against her protruding stomach. "You, the boat and that bathing suit."

A laugh bubbled up from her chest. "I don't think the designers had me in mind when they invented this skimpy thing."

His gaze warmed her all over. "It's exactly what I have in mind." He rose from where he kneeled, his hands skimming her wide girth. "I can't imagine anything sexier, more appealing, than you in that bathing suit. Now. Exactly the way you are."

His gaze captured hers as he kissed her. Eva melted against him. Had she ever felt so special in her life? So sexy? So needed? So loved? Adam's tongue explored her mouth, and she reacquainted herself with the intoxicating taste of him, knowing the answer was no.

"Yes," she whispered between kisses. She might not be able to consummate their marriage until after the baby was born, but she reveled in knowing that there were so many other ways she could satisfy him. "Oh, yes, I'll marry you, Adam Grayson. Now. Tonight. And this time it will be for more than one day. The way I see it, you have a lot to prove to me. And you're going to need a lifetime to do it." Her lips lingered on his. "It's a good thing I have that lifetime to give you."

Somewhere during his endearing proposal, Eva realized the restlessness she'd felt all day wasn't due to inactivity, but was rather the beginning of labor. "And Adam?" she asked as what was clearly a contraction surged down through her abdomen. "I, uh, I think you'd better get started right away. Because I think our daughter is anxious to join us."

Epilogue

Twenty months later

Birth Announcement

Caroline Mavros Grayson is tickled to announce—along with proud parents Adam and Eva—the birth of her little brother, Daniel Christos. Weighing in at a hefty nine pounds, five ounces, Daniel came screaming into the world at 8:05 p.m., on Thursday, December 24, during holiday festivities at the Mavros household. Proud grandparents Tolly—who helped harried second-time daddy Adam deliver the determined infant—and Katina agree that Daniel is the best Christmas gift they have ever received.

You are cordially invited to a post–New Year's Bash to help celebrate the newest addition to the Mavros and Grayson family....

ADAM PUT the extra birth announcement down on the pine dining-room table. Caroline fidgeted on his knee while he ran a callused finger along his month-old son's peach-soft cheek where he lay in the bassinet next to the table. Pure emotion surged through Adam at the thought that these two children bore his parents' first names—a Greek tradition—and his last and were a product of his and Eva's love, regardless of their genetic makeup. He tightened his arm around Caroline and nuzzled her neck, his day-end stubble eliciting a shrill giggle from the toddler.

To his right, Eva read the most recent of the RSVP's for the party next week, then closed an envelope. The quick, provocative flick of her tongue swept away Adam's paternal thoughts in exchange for far more erotic ones. She'd abandoned her heavy, red cardigan to the back of the chair, revealing the new clingy flower-print dress she wore. Her breasts, full and heavy, pressed against the material and her bare legs teased him from the generous slit in the skirt.

Adam swallowed hard. God, would the woman ever figure out how profoundly she affected him?

"Eva?"

Her green eyes shifted from the cards she had stacked on top of the laptop computer where she conducted most of the accounting associated with her home-based company. "Hmm?"

He said nothing. He didn't have to. The warm blush of color to her cheeks and her sexy little smile told him she knew exactly what he was thinking. His physical and emotional need for her skyrocketed to almost aching proportions. After nearly two years of marriage, and two children, it was amazing that he could still make his wife blush.

"Come on, Caroline," Eva said, sweeping the toddler from Adam's knee and plopping her into her playpen. "Why don't you play with your new toy for a while? Mommy and Daddy need to privately…talk about something."

Before the little girl could protest, Eva checked on the napping Daniel, then tugged Adam down the hall to their bedroom. They had built their four-bedroom ranch house on a corner of Tolly Mavros's generous land, the large bay windows of their bedroom overlooking the sleepy bayou.

Adam passionately kissed his wife, groaning when she pushed him toward the wrought-iron bed they'd filched from her old room. He fell against the mattress and Eva climbed on top of him, her womanhood cradling his painful erection as she unbuttoned the top of her dress. Adam's gaze followed the torturously slow movement, tempted to rip the fabric.... The dress finally fell away, revealing her wondrously swollen breasts.

Eva pulled the clip from her hair, and the tangled curls tumbled around her creamy shoulders. "My parents are going to be here in ten minutes, you know."

"I know," Adam grumbled, gently testing the weight of her breasts with both hands. He felt her shudder and he groaned again. Two long agonizing months had passed since he'd last made love to his wife. Sure, they had generously pursued other avenues of sexual gratification, but nothing short of a hurricane could prevent him from completely claiming her now.

"Adam?"

"Hm?" His gaze flicked up to her enchanting face.

"Are you still determined to prove your love for me?"

His throat tightened so completely he couldn't push the words through. He nodded instead.

"Then make love to me. Now."

Adam couldn't think of anything he needed to do more. And when he was finally surrounded by everything that was Eva, felt the blood pounding through his veins like a runaway locomotive, he knew that everything that had happened in his life had led to this one moment in time. He had been meant to love Eva. And Eva had been meant to love him. He caught her face in his hands, locking his gaze with hers. It was there in her eyes that he saw glistening everything he ever needed: the past, the present, the glorious future that stretched before them…and the raw proof of their love no words could ever express.

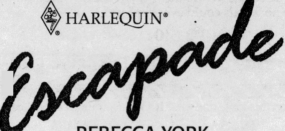